Preface

"The mission of the United States is one of benevolent assimilation."

William McKinley

Manifest Destiny – Hegemony *is a work of fiction. In writing this book, I liberally used historical persons and created other fictional characters. Any acts of these characters, whether actual or fictional, are of my imagination. Any resemblance to the actions of persons living or dead is purely* coincidental.

Books by Brian Boyington

Manifest Destiny Series:

Lincoln Sneezed

World Power

Hegemony

Unlimited Horizons

First Contact

Roman Series

Rome – An Alternative History

Acknowledgments

Editorial services for my books are completed by the on-line service Grammarly. Their services include:

1. Contextural Spelling
2. Grammar
3. Punctuation
4. Sentence Structure
5. Style
6. Vocabulary Enhancement

TABLE OF CONTENTS

Prologue

The Election of 1880.

James G Blaine, a representative from Maine, and the former Speaker of the House of Representatives, won the Republican nomination on the first ballot. Senator John Sherman, from Ohio, won the nomination for Vice President, defeating James Garfield, also from Ohio. Sherman was considered a moderate, and not aligned with either the Stalwart or Half Breed sections of the party.

The Democrat Convention nominated Winfield Scott Hancock on the first ballot. His running mate Samuel J Randall also won the Vice Presidential nomination on the first ballot.

There was little difference between the Republicans and Democrats. Both had factions favoring high tariffs, and the Gold Standard. Republican voters usually included Northern Protestants and Blacks. The Democrats often included Southern Protestants and Northern Catholics. Citizens in Ontario were predominately Protestant Republicans. Citizens in Quebec were predominately Catholic but were fiercely loyal to the Parti-Patriote. The Party-Patriot considered themselves to be Independents in Congress and depending on the issue sided with either the Republicans or the Democrats.

On November 2, the polls opened, and 78% of the voters cast ballots. The vote count gave the Blaine Ticket 4,956,501 votes. The Hancock Ticket received 4,560,410 votes. The Electoral College was more lopsided, providing Blaine with 233 Electoral Votes and Hancock 155. The Republicans also regained control of both Houses of Congress.

President-elect Blaine reflected on the events of the past 20 years. He was elected in 1861 to the United States House of Representatives, from the Maine third district. His skill in Congress was instrumental gathering support for Abraham Lincoln's proposed Thirteenth Amendment, and he worked tirelessly to win a two-thirds majority for the Amendment in the House.

He was an ardent supporter of President Lincoln's efforts to provide amnesty to Confederate leaders. These efforts assisted in the reunification of the nation following four years of Civil War. His political skills catapulted him to his election as Speaker of the House in 1868.

During the war with Great Britain in 1868 and 1869, he used his influence as Speaker to provide support for the war effort, which led to the defeat of Great Britain and the annexation of Canada, Bermuda and the Bahamas.

He was present at the reviewing station seated next to Vice President Grant during the celebratory parades following the passage of the Fifteenth Amendment. He witnessed the grenade attack, which assassinated President Lincoln. As Speaker of the House, he rode on the funeral train during it's a long journey to Springfield, Illinois.

In 1874 Blaine was an ardent supporter of President Grant during the Spanish-American War. As Speaker of the House, Blaine guaranteed that monies were allocated to support the war effort. Following the Peace of Paris on May 1, 1874, the United States formally annexed Cuba and Puerto Rico.

He led the *Half-breed faction* of the Republican Party and opposed President Grant for the nomination in 1876. He won over forty percent of the delegates and extracted promises of reforms from the President before giving Grant his support.

Three days after the convention, Blaine was appointed to the United States Senate to fill the vacancy left by Senator Lott Morrell, who vacated the Post to be Secretary of the Treasury. Reconfirmed by the Maine State Senate, Blaine served as Senator until elected President in 1880.

When the new Congress convened on December 7, 1880, it faced a new decade with fresh challenges. Cuba and Puerto had elected non-voting representatives to Congress. Naval bases were under expansion at Samana Bay in Domenica and Pearl Harbor in the Kingdom of Hawaii. With strong naval forces on both coasts, a canal through Central America became a necessity. President-Elect Blaine favored future expansion. With Manifest Destiny realized on the North American Continent and the Caribbean, what would the new decade bring?

Chapter 1

On March 4, 1881, following President Blaine's inauguration, several gala receptions were held. At one of the receptions receiving lines, Blaine met the Consul General to Liberia, John Smyth who asked for an appointment to discuss pressing Liberian issues. President Blaine agreed and requested his Chief of Staff, John Edwards, to set up a meeting the following week.

At 2 pm on March 11, Consul General John Smyth arrived for his appointment with President Blaine. He met with John Edwards and Secretary of State James Garfield. Together the three of them entered the Oval Office. President Blaine's schedule was full, so he quickly asked John Smyth what was so urgent in Liberia.

Recognizing the President's mood, Smyth went directly to the point. "Mr. President, Liberia, over the past six years has actively extended its borders to the Niger River in the north, occupying the unclaimed territory between British-ruled Sierra Leone and French-ruled Ivory Coast. Initially, this was to accommodate increased immigration of United States blacks into Liberia. While that was the truth, another reason has surfaced. There are numerous diamond and mineral discoveries in that area. Liberia intends to exploit those resources by populating and annexing that territory. Their army has already established several forts in the area.

News like that is impossible to suppress for long, and a diamond rush is in the making. Liberian troops are patrolling their side of the borders on each side, and are turning back the French and British prospectors. Both the British and French chargé d'affaires have lodged protests at my office in Monrovia, and are threatening severe consequences if the current situation persists. I bought us some time by promising them I would meet with you.

Before leaving Liberia, I presented my

diplomatic credentials to the new President Charles Taylor. If you remember, he was the overall commander of Liberian forces during the British incursion of "67." I expressed the British and French concerns. He replied that Liberia has been populating the area for the past six-years without protest and previously annexed much of the territory before the discoveries. He indicated that Liberia could accommodate individual foreign miners, but would not tolerate international corporations exploiting the resources.

Secretary of State Garfield asked: "Can Liberia withstand the British and French pressure"?

Smyth replied: "Their army is undoubtedly the strongest native army on the continent. The commanding officer is Major General Obadiah Driver. He is a former Sergeant Major of the Massachusetts 54th regiment. He is also the one who led their ground forces at the Battle of Amina. He pulled off a double-envelopment of the British Army, forcing its surrender.

Their senior officers are professionals, seasoned in battle. Many of their junior officers are West Point graduates. President Grant opened the Academy enrollment to Liberians in “72.” Both of General Driver’s sons are West Point Graduates. Before entering politics, General Taylor established The East Point Military Academy in Liberia; and modeled it after West Point. Liberia has hired many former West Point instructors. General Driver has continued that policy, plus some of his veteran officers are also instructors.

However, the fortifications protecting Monrovia at Fort Monroe and Fort Clay are obsolete. The existing Parrot Rifles are ineffective against modern warships, and naval gunnery has surpassed the Parrot Rifles in range and accuracy. These fortifications would not survive a sustained bombardment.”

Edwards then asked: “Do they have other

military resources"?

Smyth answered: "They have a small Navy. Their naval assets are primarily for coastal defense. We sold them, five Canonicus Monitors in 1870. The upgrades to these vessels included a new turret with twin eight-inch long guns. Two of the upgraded Canonicus Monitors are protecting the entrance to Lake Piso and Bomi. The other three are guarding Monrovia. Their eight-inch cannons could defend against cruisers but would have minimal effectiveness against battleships.

With our help, they converted the captured HMS, now LRS Glorious to a twin-turreted monitor similar to our Agamenticus class warships. Like the Agamenticus Class ships, LRS Glorious has two turrets, each with twin eleven-inch-long guns." She is patrolling the East Africa coast to guard against persistent pirate raids on their commercial shipping. Her officers are former United States Navy personnel who moved to Liberia for financial gain.

Coincidentally, there has been consistent cooperation with both the Royal Navy and French Navy in raiding pirate bases. LRS Glorious's long guns reduce the pirate strongholds, while Royal Navy and French Marines force their landings."

Garfield then spoke up. "There is a pathway open for negotiations between the Liberians, the British and the French. There are mutual advantages for all three nations. The European powers are involved in significant colonialization of Africa. Liberia will need our support to stay independent. If we offer our services to facilitate an agreement, we could prevent a war in West Africa. The British and the French are unlikely to press for a forced agreement if they know we are involved."

Then looking at President Blaine, he continued: "Mr. President, I suggest we send cables to both the British and French governments, expressing our growing concern regarding their implied threats of serious consequences directed at Liberia. I will suggest a conference be scheduled here in Washington DC, or at a neutral capital city of their choice. Negotiations, not war should settle this issue."

President Blaine agreed. Addressing Garfield, he stated: "Liberia is our protectorate, and we will not tolerate foreign interference in her affairs. We will re-direct the British and French aspirations into other areas of Africa. The United States only interest on that continent is to ensure Liberian independence. Make sure the British and the French are aware of our position

Then addressing John Smyth, President Blaine said: "Set up a meeting with the Liberian Plenipotentiary and explain to him our position. Liberia, the British and the French need to agree on defined borders. We will assist in determining fair and defensible borders." Hastily writing a memo, Blaine handed it to Smyth. "Take this to the Secretary of the Army Robert Lincoln. Ask him to organize a team of engineers to modify the Liberian defenses at Forts Monroe and Clay that they be able to accommodate long guns."

John Smyth thanked the President for the memo, and Secretary of State Garfield and Chief of Staff John Edwards for their time and attention. Smyth then excused himself from the meeting. Secretary of the Navy Porter then was introduced and entered.

The next order of business was Peru's offer to lease Chimbote Bay to the United States. Chimbote Bay would provide the United States a naval base in a deepwater Pacific port in South America.

Secretary Garfield began his explanation. Peru and Bolivia recently suffered defeat by Chile in the War of the Pacific. Both Peru and Bolivia lost substantial portions of their territory. Bolivia lost their western provinces and access to the Pacific Ocean. Peru lost its southernmost region. Fearing their new and aggressive southern neighbor, Peru sought a close alliance with the United

States. Leasing Chimbote Bay to the United States would form such a partnership.

However, rumors of the lease proposal leaked out to Chile, which took action. First, the Chilean Ambassador to the United States met with me, and protested, citing the presence of a United States Naval base in Peru was a direct threat to their sovereignty. I assured them that the United States has no territorial ambitions in that area. Apparently, he did not accept my explanation. Last week, Chile dispatched 750 marines, and a naval expedition to occupy the bay. Previously the Peruvian inhabitants lived in small fishing villages. The civilians are now forced to serve the Chilean military.

Informed of the occupation of Chimbote Bay, I summoned the Chilean Ambassador and warned him that Chile must evacuate or face the consequences of their aggression. Secure in their dominant position in South America, and with a peace treaty with

Argentina ending their border war, the Chilean Ambassador rejected what he considered our bullying. The Chilean government is confident that the United States will be reluctant to go to war with Chile for so little, and so far from our shores."

President Blaine, addressing Secretary of the Navy Porter, asked: " What Naval assets do we have to impress the Chileans to end their occupation? Our naval display must be of sufficient stature to impress them of their folly."

Porter replied: "Mr. President, Admiral Kincaid has five Puritan Class Monitors, plus USS Monadnock, and escorts at the Mare Island Naval Base in San Francisco. He could be available to expel the Chilean Naval task force and Marines from Chimbote Bay. His fleet will be ready for deployment within one week. There are transports available to carry two-thousand Marines with the fleet."

Checking his notes, Secretary Porter continued. Admiral Lee's fleet has previously scheduled exercises in the Carribean to test the effectiveness of the improvements on USS Indiana. Those exercises could be planned further south, off the Brazillian coast, possibly adjacent the Rio de la Plata to send a message to the Brazilians and the Argentines. Argentina has a long border with Chile and both dispute the sovereignty of Patagonia. Up to now, the Argentines only have a brown water navy. With the commissioning of our new battleships, the older Agamenticus Class monitors will become expendable. We could offer to sell them to the Argentine Navy.

Garfield added: "We could honor Brazil's Emperor Pedro II Fiftieth Jubilee with a parade of warships in Rio de Janeiro. I could personally present a gift from the people of the United States of America. That would provide us with a plausible reason for our naval presence and the subsequent war games. We could also arrange a goodwill visit to Buenos Aries."

With diplomacy at a standstill, President Blaine agreed with the plan. Blaine ordered Secretary Perry to dispatch of Admiral Lee and his fleet, now including the USS Indiana as his flagship south to attend the Jubilee for Pedro II, then hold the naval exercises in full view of Argentina. His mission was to solidify relations with the Empire of Brazil and to impress the Argentines the value of a strong relationship with the United States. If war broke out with Chile, Lee would steam through the Straits of Magellan into the Pacific.

Admiral Kincaid's instructions were to lead his Puritan Class Monitors and escorts south from San Francisco and expel the Chilean Naval task force and Marines from Chimbote Bay. The hope was that the show of force would cause the Chileans to retreat. If the Chileans chose war, they would suffer the consequences.

The last subject of business was the Civil

War in Columbia. President Blaine asked Garfield to provide an update on that situation.

Garfield responded: “Mr. President, the fighting started in 1876 over public education. The radical liberal government, led by Aquileo Para y Gomez, tried to institute public education. The conservatives, backed by the Catholic Church, wanted the teaching done by Catholic parochial schools.

Fighting developed between rival liberal and conservative generals. The Liberal Party also split when forces loyal to Gomez’s moderate rival Rafael Nunez threw their support to the Conservatives. Sporadic fighting continued for four years. In the election of 1880, the alliance of Nunez and the conservatives won, with Nunez elected President.

Protesting what they believed to be corrupt elections, the liberal backers of Aquileo Para y Gomez refused to accept the results and rioted in the streets. The instability escalated when rioters in Cartagena took over the city and took foreign nationals, including the United States Consul hostage; and imprisoned them in the Castillo San Felipe De Barajas. The crisis deepened, when the soldiers sent by the Para y Gomez government refused to suppress the rioters and joined the revolution."

President Blaine asked Secretary Perry what assets were available in the area to free the hostages.

Perry replied: "Admiral Treat's base of operation is Samana Bay. He is conducting fleet exercises in the Bay, including a practice of an amphibious landing with General Grissom's Buffalo Soldiers. His forces could be in Cartegena within three days."

President Blaine responded: "Excellent, order Admiral Treat to sail to Cartegena and rescue the hostages. Looking long-term, we might be able to use our assistance to gain favor with the Nunez government for our proposal to construct a canal through their northern province of Panama." With the afternoon's agenda cleared, President Blaine adjourned the meeting.

Secretary Perry cabled the Admiral's orders. In Samana Bay, following two days of activity re-coaling his vessels, and provisioning the troopships, Admiral Treat, aboard USS Puritan, in company with troopships carrying a brigade of Buffalo Soldiers, led his fleet out of Samana Bay, and set course for Cartegena.

Admiral Kincaid followed similar procedures making preparations at Mare Island. Five days later, his fleet saluted East Point and Alcatraz as they steamed through the Golden Gate.

On March 19, Secretary of State Garfield boarded USS Indiana at Hampton Roads. Garfield stood on the bridge with Admiral Lee as his fleet steamed out of Hampton

Roads. Following the departure, Garfield briefed Admiral Lee of the full mission goals.

Chapter 2

Cartagena, Columbia.

March 18, 1881.

Admiral Treat's fleet steamed to Cartagena. The city faced west, with a wall protecting the shoreline approach. The only open entrance was the Boca Chica channel. Castillo de Boca Chica guarded the passage on the land side, and a boom extended across the inlet to a separate battery on the facing peninsula. The State Department had notified the Para y Gomez government that the fleet was approaching. Para y Gomez was warned to release the hostages or the United States forces would occupy the city.

Forces loyal to the Nunez faction had already invested the city, and there was sporadic fighting with the rebels, and renegade Para y Gomez forces who occupied the Castillo San Felipe De

Barajas. The rebels held the old walled city, The Castillo de Boca Chica, and the Castillo San Felipe De Barajas.

The Nunez forces had surrounded Castillo San Felipe and were negotiating with the commander for the surrender of the hostages. They also laid siege to the rebels holding the city. The arrival of Treat's fleet and transports brought the simmering cauldron to a boil.

USS Puritan entered the Boca Chica Channel, heading towards the waterfront. The fort's commander ordered a warning shot across Puritan's bow. Captain Decatur maintained the course. However, he ordered the rotation of his 12" long guns towards the Castillo. The Castillo's guns then fired on USS Puritan, which replied with four devastating salvos blasting the Castillo's ramparts, resulting in the partial collapse of the walls. The next warships in line, USS Agementicus, USS Towanda, and USS Sangamon also fired salvos into the Castillo, collapsing more of the walls and silencing the guns. With the Castillo in ruins, the surviving defenders surrendered, and those defending the port retreated into the walled city.

The troop transports followed the warships and docked at the port. Major Hannibal Johnson led the first battalion of General Grissom's Buffalo Soldiers as they captured the piers. Hannibal's men quickly secured the port and penetrated several blocks into the warehouse area surrounding the harbor. Hannibal supervised the preparation of defensive positions to prevent interference from the walled city.

An officer leading a detachment of Columbian Army soldiers met the lead elements of the Buffalo Soldiers. The officer identified himself as Captain Raphael Ramirez and offered Colombian Army assistance in capturing Castillo San Felipe. The company commander, Captain Peter Jones sent a squad of soldiers to escort Captain Ramirez to Hannibal.

Hannibal greeted Ramirez, then sent a messenger to General Grissom that a Columbian Army officer was present, and offered to liaison with American soldiers to capture the Castillo. Within an hour, General Grissom appeared with his other battalion commanders. He and his battalion commanders met with Ramirez at Hannibal's office in a vacant storefront.

Ramirez revealed that his commanding officer Colonel Alfonso Carrillo invested the Castillo with 2500 soldiers. However, they lacked heavy weaponry and were reluctant to attack a garrison firmly established in the fortifications. Ramirez did reveal that he had previously been stationed at the Castillo, and had a map including hidden passageways. He produced this map from his shoulder bag. He spread the document out on a table. General Grissom and his officers gathered around the table. Ramirez pointed out vulnerabilities in the defenses, and interior passages which would provide attackers a method to circumvent the defensive positions.

Castillo San Felipe De Barajas

The rebel commandant Colonel Esteban Gomez y Mareno watched in trepidation as the United States warships destroyed Castillo Boca Chica. He understood that his fortifications were over 100 years old and would not survive such a bombardment. He also watched as United States soldiers began to advance towards the Castello. Within a matter of hours, he could anticipate an assault. Meeting with his officers, he outlined his plan.

Colonel Mareno began: "I proposed an armistice with the Columbian soldiers laying siege to the Castillo. Our rebellion is over. We have one opportunity to save ourselves. In return for our freedom, we will release all the hostages. Time is running out to make this agreement. Up to this time, sporadic firing between the besiegers and us has only caused minor wounds. Once the Americans fully deploy the opportunity will be gone. Are you with me on this? Who can I count on to take the message to Colonel Carrillo? The Colonel and I were soldiers together. He will listen to reason."

One of his officers, a strident advocate for the revolution spoke up. "Colonel this is madness. We hold the hostages as poker chips. If the Americans attack, we will kill all the hostages and the first will be their Consul. I will die before surrendering our advantage." The other officers looked shocked then began to grumble amongst themselves. Colonel Mareno, realizing that drastic action was required, pulled out his sidearm and shot the officer three times in the chest. Shaking his head, Mareno said: "Esteban you were always a hothead, there I granted your wish." Then, while looking at the officers, he said: "I still need that volunteer."

One hour later, the gate at Castillo San Felipe opened, and a single horseman carrying a white flag rode towards the besieging Columbian lines. Three horsemen met him, and after being informed, he had a message for Colonel Alfonso Carrillo, they escorted him to the Colonel's headquarters. He was searched for weapons and asked for identification. Then, he was accompanied by two armed guards into the office, where they presented him to Carrillo as Captain Fulgent Bautista. The guards then stood at parade rest, blocking the door.

Without preamble, Colonel Carrillo said: "Captain state your business, are you here to surrender"? Captain Bautista saluted and stated: "Sir, compliments of Colonel Gomez y Mareno, he asked me to present this letter to you." Looking at the guards, he said: "If I may," then he reached into his breast pocket and pulled out a sealed letter. Bautista handed the message to the guard, who in turn gave it to Colonel Carrillo. Carrillo broke the seal, opened the document, and began reading.

Colonel Alfonso Carrillo:

My Friend, it is with great distress and regrets that I find this letter necessary. President Gomez y Gomez ordered me to Cartagena to free the hostages. I implore you to believe me that obeying those orders was my sincerest intent. However, upon arriving, I discovered that my directions were an impossible task as our enemies outnumbered my regiment by three to one.

To save my regiment and the hostages, I pretended to join the rebellion and took custody of the hostages and remanded them to the safest place in Cartagena, the Castillo San Felipe.

Now that the Americans have arrived, and the rebels are contained in the city, I can fulfill my duty and release the hostages to your custody. I assure you, the hostages have been well cared for, and are in good health. As a demonstration of faith, the gates of the Castillo will remain open to you.

I remain,

Colonel Esteban Gomez y Mareno

Looking up from his desk, Carrillo stared intently into the Captain's eyes. The letter offered an opportunity to rescue the hostages without a costly battle which would endanger the hostage's lives. He knew Colonel Mareno well, and at one time they were close friends.

Making his decision, he said: "Captain, return to Colonel Mareno. I accept his offer to release the hostages. I will communicate your offer and my acceptance with our American allies. I am sure they will wish to take custody of the hostages, particularly their Consul."

Captain Bautista saluted, turned on his heel and marched out of the building. As he rode back to the Castillo, he saw a long column of the Buffalo Soldiers marching into Colonel Carrillo's camp. Spurring his horse forward, he thought to himself *The Colonel was correct, we were out of time.*

General Grissom, Hannibal, and the 2nd Batallion Commander, Major Samuel Jefferson were riding at the head of the column of the Buffalo Soldiers. The sight of the Columbian officer as he spurred his horse to the Castillo drew Grissom's attention. Hannibal following the general's gaze noted that the gates of the Castillo were open, and pointed in that direction. Grissom grunted then said to his officers: "I suspect that a deal to free the hostages is in the works. Let's find out what Colonel Carrillo has to offer."

Colonel Carrillo, hearing the column arriving, walked out onto the front porch of his office. After he and General Grissom had exchanged salutes, Grissom introduced Hannibal and Major Jefferson. Carrillo then led the way into his office. After providing refreshments and enjoying cigars, Carrillo handed Colonel Mareno's note to General Grissom, who read it twice, then passed it onto Hannibal, who then gave it to

Jefferson.

Grissom spoke: “Do you believe what this Colonel Mareno has written? To me, the letter looks opportunistic.”

Carrillo laughed, then agreed. “Mareno is a survivor. I have known him for years, and he has strong liberal tendencies. Your Navy's arrival and their destruction of the Castillo Boca Chica opened his eyes. Your occupation of the port facilities ended his gambit. He exercised his only other option to escape the gallows. However, he has provided us with the opportunity to secure the hostages without further bloodshed. His life spared, and the hostages released. A fair exchange.”

Grissom inquired: What about the walled city; the rebels are still in control. More importantly, do you need our assistance in driving them out”?

Carrillo replied: “The hostage release fulfills your obligations. Capturing the city will be an internal matter. However, a display of naval artillery support could be helpful in the resolution. I will offer them a chance to surrender. If they refuse, the reduction of a portion of the walls will allow us entry into the city. I will provide Colonel Mareno's regiment the honor of leading the assault. Your presence should inspire him to perform his duties."

Grissom smiled, then replied: I will confer with the Admiral. His agreement will be essential. My immediate concern is taking custody of the hostages." Turning to Hannibal Grissom continued: "Major, prepare a squad and an officer to take my message to the Admiral about the pending release of the hostages. Once I have them in my custody, I will personally escort them to the fleet." There I can meet with the Admiral and discuss our plans. This plan can be mutually advantageous.

Speaking to Colonel Carrillo, Grissom said: "Please contact Colonel Mareno. It is vitally important that I meet with our Consul to determine the status of their captivity." Carrillo readily agreed and dispatched Captain Ramirez with an escort to the Castillo.

One hour later Ramirez and his escort returned leading a wagon train containing the hostages. Riding next to Ramirez was the American Consul Isaiah James. While Carrillo and his staff attended to the hostages, Counsel James and General Grissom secluded themselves in Carrillo's office.

There the Consul largely confirmed Mareno's account. He began: "During the riots, the rebels gathered up and jailed all the foreigners they could find. When they came to the Consulate, our police guards either fled or cooperated with the rioters.

The rioters hung my Columbian staff in my presence, placed a noose around my neck, and dragged me out to the street. Then burned the Consulate, beat me senseless, and threw me into the back of a wagon. I woke up in a rat-infested cell. Days later, after several of my fellow captives died, Colonel Mareno arrived and talked the rioters into confining us into the Castillo. He told them that we were not worth anything if we were dead.

Once at the Castillo, we received medical care, provided with baths and clean clothes. We were still prisoners but were well treated. There was one officer who insulted and threatened us continuously. I understand that the Colonel personally executed him. Make no mistake; I am not absolving the Colonel for imprisoning us. What he did was make our imprisonment survivable."

General Grissom listened intently until Consul James finished. He then said: "Your treatment by the rebels is intolerable. I need to take you to Admiral Treat. The guns on his vessels can reduce the city walls to make an assault possible. The rebel leaders must face punishment for their actions." Consul James agreed. He and

General Grissom, escorted by a company of Buffalo Soldiers rode to the port and boarded a longboat which took them to USS Puritan. After hearing Consul James' story, Admiral Treat agreed to bombard the walls before an assault on the walled city.

The next morning, Colonels Carillo and Mareno assembled their troops on the land side of the walled city. A messenger under a flag of truce delivered an ultimatum requiring them to surrender or die. The rebels replied by shooting the messenger as he rode back to the Columbian lines. Carrillo ordered a red rocket fired, the signal for Admiral Treat's warships to open fire.

USS Puritan opened fire with a salvo from the four twelve-inch guns. Immediately the other warships in the fleet fired their salvos. Each shell hitting the wall tore out chunks of masonry. After 30-minutes of the bombardment, whole sections of the wall collapsed, causing significant breaches. The cannon fire continued walking into the city, igniting numerous fires.

Protected by the bombardment, the Columbian troops surged forward, through the breaches, into the city. After two hours of fierce fighting, the walled portion of Cartagena fell. The surviving rebel leaders were led out, lined up in front of the wall and executed by firing squad. Isolated, rebel pockets of resistance fought bravely to the end. None surrendered.

USS Dispatch left for Hampton Roads with the report of the victory. With the city secured, Admiral Treat and General Grissom planned to return to Samana Bay. A telegraph message from Bogata arrived inviting Admiral Treat, Consul James, and General Grissom to the inauguration of President Nunez. USS Dispatch returned with a letter appointing Consul James to Ambassador.

Chapter 3

March 28, 1881.

Chimbote Bay.

Two weeks after departing San Francisco, Admiral Kincaid's flagship the *USS Kearsarge* led a fleet of five Puritan Class monitors to within 50 nautical miles northwest of Chimbote Bay, Peru. Kincaid's. His warships steamed in a spread V formation with *USS Kearsarge* on point. Sister ships *USS Winslow* and *USS Atlas* steamed on the starboard flank, and *USS Satyr* and *USS Mercury* on the port flank. The troopships and collier ships held station in the middle. Two frigates and four sloops of war formed a layered scouting screen extending fifteen miles ahead.

The sloops-of-war *USS Astor* and *USS Pegasus* were the lead scout ships, stationed three miles apart, with *USS Astor* one mile astern. The masthead lookout on

USS Pegasus sighted smoke on the horizon and signaled am *investigating.* USS Astor relayed the signal back to the fleet and steamed forward to assist *USS Pegasus*. Within an hour Pegasus identified the approaching vessel as the Chilean ironclad turret ship *Huascar*, with two escorts. Signaling *enemy in sight, Pegasus* came about steaming back towards *USS Astor* and the fleet.

The *Huascar*, a twin-turreted monitor, was originally a Peruvian warship, constructed in 1868 for Peru by Great Britain at the Laird Shipyard. As-built, her armored protection consisted of 5 ½ inches of wrought-iron plates over a Teak wood hull. Huascar's turrets each had two 10-inch Armstrong rifled muzzle-loading cannons and a Gatling gun. *Almiralte Cochrane* captured her during the War of the Pacific at the Battle of Angamos. Following extensive repairs, and the removal of the fore-mast, Huascar was commissioned into the Chilean Navy.

Huascar, escorted by two, twenty-gun

corvettes increased steam to pursue *USS Pegasus*. The Corvettes surged ahead to overtake the escaping sloop-of-war, then sighted *USS Astor* with signal flags flying. The Pursuit continued for another thirty minutes until the two United States Navy 36-gun frigates, *USS Spectre* and *USS Sword* appeared over the horizon steaming at full speed to aid their smaller consorts. Each mounted six, 15-inch Parrot Rifles on the main deck, and thirty, 32-pound cannons, 15 to a side of the gun deck. Captain George Dewey ordered *USS Spectre*, to close with the Corvettes, While Captain Thayer Mahan steamed *USS Sword* towards *Huascar. The fleeing USS Astor* and *USS Pegasus* came about and followed the frigates into battle. Each mounted three, 15-inch Parrot Rifles, and four 32-pound cannons.

The Chilean and United States ships were three miles apart when waterspouts from incoming shells exploded one-half mile forward of the Chilean warships. Realizing they were almost in range of United States

Naval long guns, the *Huascar* and her two consorts came about and fled south towards Chimbote Bay. The USS warships shortened sail and slowed the steam engines, waiting for Admiral Kincaid to catch up. One hour later the Puritan Class Monitors arrived, and Admiral Kincaid signaled *Captain's repair on-board.*

Admiral Kincaid held the captain's conference in the wardroom of *USS Kearsarge*. He began the meeting welcoming his captains to the wardroom. He then stated: The Chileans know we are here, and that we have come in force. Maybe our demonstration of firepower will motivate them to depart Chimbote Bay in peace. If they do not offer battle, I am inclined to let them leave. In case they do decide to fight, we will first have to eliminate their corvettes and any torpedo boats, then take on their ironclads. If the Chileans offer battle, here is the action plan. Following the meeting, the captains returned to their warships to prepare them for their next day's arrival at Chimbote Bay and potential battle.

The next morning at 9 am, Admiral Kincaid paraded his warships from north to south in front of Chimbote Bay, then came about and repeated the process from south to north. Signal flags broke out above *USS Kearsarge* signaling *USS Spectre* to raise the international black flag for parley and enter Chimbote Bay. With gun ports closed and the parley flag flying from the foremast, Captain Dewey steamed *USS Spectre* into the bay verifying the number and type of Chilean warships.

Captain Charles Condell de LaHaza on *Almiralte Cochrane* ordered the black parley flag flown, and signaled Captain Dewey an invitation to come aboard. A lieutenant met Dewey at the rail, piped him aboard, and escorted him to Captain Condell's quarters where he handed Condell a letter from Admiral Kincaid and a copy of the ninety-nine-year lease agreement between Peruvian President Nicholas Pierola and the United States.

After reading the letter and lease agreement, Condell stated: "We do not recognize Pierola as President of Peru as he seized power in a Coup. A signed peace treaty between Chile and Peru does not exist. Therefore we are still at war. We took Chimbote Bay in that war and will either keep it or use it as a negotiating chip during any peace agreement." Tossing Admiral Kincaid's letter and the lease agreement across the table, Condell continued: "Chile does not recognize the validity of this lease agreement, and we will not surrender this valuable asset to the United States."

Dewey, sensing that there was nothing else to discuss, stood up to leave. He stated: Captain Condell, I urge you to reconsider. We have more and larger ships and out-gun your vessels. To stand and fight will be futile, and will only result in the loss of your warships and men. I will bring your reply back to Admiral Kincaid. The decision will be his. However, the consequences will be yours." With that, Dewey saluted and left, boarded his longboat back to *USS Spectre* which steamed out of the bay back to the Admiral Kincaid's fleet.

Admiral Kincaid signaled *USS Spectre – Captain repair on-board.* Dewey ordered his ship to steam close on the flagship; then he boarded his longboat to be rowed to *USS Kearsarge*. Kincaid requested a full report. Dewey informed Kincaid that he observed Chilean had the *Almiralte Cochrane, the Huascar,* and two corvettes. He also reported that he did not see any of the dangerous torpedo boats. However, they could have been concealed behind the corvettes. Dewey then repeated his conversation with Captain Condell and the probability that the Chileans would fight.

Kincaid then asked: "How formidable a warship is the *Almiralte Cochrane*."

Dewey replied: "She is a British built ironclad, and her inner hull is all-metal construction. Captain Condell's cabin had all-metal walls. She is a battery warship with three main guns and two smaller ones in the amidships battery on both sides. The main guns look to be nine to 10 inches. She appears to have a reinforced armored belt on both sides. She would be formidable in single combat and was responsible for the capture of *Huascar* from the Peruvian Navy. Two of our Puritan Class warships should be able to defeat her. *Huascar* is an older monitor style warship and should not be a significant challenge to our fleet."

Admiral Kincaid then asked: "Did you see *Almiralte Cochrane's* sister ship the *Blanco Encalada*"? Dewey replied: "She was not in the bay. However, I suspect she is lurking someplace close and will engage once our ships are committed. That would explain why Captain Condell was willing to engage against overwhelming odds."

Kincaid then said: "George, stay on-board." Then to his flag lieutenant, he said: "Signal to all Captain's *Repair on-board*. Then speaking to Dewey, he said: "It will take time for them to arrive. You served under John Winslow. What kind of man was he, and what was it like to serve under him"? Dewey recounted his three years as an Executive Officer on the original *USS Kearsarge*, and her final battle at Bermuda; when the severely wounded Captain John Winslow went down with his ship.

Kincaid thanked Dewey for his dramatic re-telling of the story. He then stated: "The Navy will always remember John for his ingenuity and courage. They honored him with his posthumous promotion to Admiral, and increased that honor by naming USS Kearsarge's sister ship after him."

Minutes later, the Captains arrived, and Kincaid laid out his plan of action. He cautioned his captains against overconfidence. He reminded them that the *Almiralte Cochrane and Blanco Encalada* were formidable opponents and that the Chilean Navy had recently experienced victories over warships from Bolivia and Peru.

Chapter 4

March 30, 1881.

Admiral Lee's fleet steamed into Rio de Janeiro, situated inside Guanabana Bay. The crew in dress uniforms lined the decks as each ship fired salutes to Forts Santa Cruz, Sao Jao, Lajos, and Villegaignon. Fireworks erupted from the dozens of other nations warships anchored in the bay gathered to celebrate the 50th Jubilee of Emperor Pedro II. Guard boats escorted the fleet to mooring anchorages in the bay, and gaily decorated steamboats surrounded the warships to provide passage for shore leave.

A special diplomatic steamboat moored next to USS Indiana. Minister Plenipotentiary Henry Hilliard greeted Secretary of State Garfield, Admiral Lee and Captain Powell. Together, and with an entourage of aides in a separate boat, the diplomatic party were escorted to the palace dock.

A Majo Domo escorted Garfield, Hilliard, Lee, and Powell into the palace for their scheduled audience with the Emperor. Two footmen in brightly colored livery carried an ornate chest bearing the gifts for Pedro II. Other footmen escorted the entourage to another reception chamber.

Pedro II warmly greeted the diplomatic party from the United States. Plenipotentiary Hilliard introduced them one by one. Secretary of State Garfield then spoke.

"Your Highness, President Blaine, on behalf of the people of the United States of America, presents you these gifts on your Fiftieth Jubilee These gifts are meant to symbolize the bonds of friendship between the United States of America and the Empire of Brazil."

He then gestured to the two footmen who brought the chest forward, placed it on a table and opened it for the Emperor. Inside were busts of George Washington,

Abraham Lincoln, and scroll copies of the Declaration of Independence, and Lincoln's Second Inaugural Address.

The gifts significantly moved Pedro II, who revered his father Pedro I for leading Brazil's independence movement in 1823, and was an admirer of George Washington and Abraham Lincoln. He said: "On behalf of the citizens of the Empire of Brazil, I accept these gifts and the bonds of friendship they represent."

Garfield replied: "Your Highness, President Blaine would like to solidify relations between the United States and the Empire of Brazil. Minister Hilliard is eager to work with your government agencies to explore means of cooperation."

Pedro II smiled broadly at the suggestion then said: "In due time, We will have to arrange these meetings He then gestured his guests to follow him into the grand reception hall where his court laid out a gala banquet for all the visiting dignitaries.

Garfield, Hilliard, Lee, and Powell mixed freely with the other diplomats and military representatives. Garfield met with the Ambassador of the United Kingdom Sir Francis Clare Ford. Ambassador Ford expressed some diplomatic disbelief at Garfield's explanation of why the United States sent such a strong fleet to participate in Pedro II 50th Jubilee boat parade.

Garfield chuckled and replied: The United States desires to demonstrate that we are a reliable and dependable ally, whose purpose is to provide stability in the region. We just confirmed that fact in Columbia. The intervention of our Naval assets resulted in the crushing of the Cartegena revolution. We secured the release of all the diplomatic hostages, including your Consul. Our fleet then provided logistic and naval gun support to the Columbian Army as they recaptured Cartegena. That enabled their freely elected government to assume power.

Our new Ambassador Isaiah James was present for the inauguration of President Nunez who expressed his thanks for our assistance. With its task completed our naval fleet departed with the repatriated diplomatic personnel. Unlike the European powers, the United States has no colonial ambitions. It is in our best interest to facilitate stable governments in our neighbor nations. Then as friends and neighbors, we can develop mutually profitable relations."

Ambassador Ford was unconvinced, but for Machiavellian purposes congratulated Garfield for the successful campaign in Columbia. He ended the conversation by stating.

"I am sure that you will succeed in profitable ventures in Columbia. However, only the future will determine how mutually beneficial it will be for the Columbians." With that, he shook Garfield's hand and moved on to the reception.

Admiral Lee was meeting with his Royal

Navy counterpart Vice-Admiral Sir F. L. McClintock who was commander of the West Indies Fleet based in Jamaica. McClintock's flagship was the armored cruiser HMS Northampton, which was moored ½ mile from USS Indiana. Lee invited McClintock to tour USS Indiana and to be a guest during the scheduled fleet maneuvers. McClintock agreed. The transfer would take place following the parade of ships, which would commence the following day.

The Parade of ships was uneventful. Naval vessels from Brazil led the formation. Each ship fired a salute as it steamed past the Emperor's reviewing stand. Following at the standard distance of 2,000 yards were the warships from the United States led by USS Indiana, followed by USS Massachusetts, USS Onondaga, USS Tecumseh, USS Weehawken, USS Miantonoth, USS Towanda and USS Sangamon. Warships from the United Kingdom, France, and Portugal comprised the balance of the parade.

The next morning, the United States warships departed. Admiral McClintock boarded USS Indiana with due ceremony. He accompanied Admiral Lee and Captain Powell on a tour of the vessel which included the two twelve-inch gun turrets, four six-inch turrets.

McClintock was impressed with a demonstration of the breech-loading of the guns. He commented that the Royal Navy was installing very similar weapons on their newest Battleships. Admiral Lee wryly commented: “The Germans adopted our design. Your designers have learned from them.” McClintock laughed heartily and said: “Admiral, all is fair in love and war.” Lee and Powell chuckled in assent.

The next morning the fleet maneuvers began off the south coast of Brazil. The warships of the other nations followed the United States Fleet as observers. The Argentine Ambassador, Juan Carlos DeFilippo was an observer aboard HMS

Northhampton.

The maneuvers began with USS Indiana on the port side a formation called *Line Abreast*. This formation placed the warships parallel to each other, separated by two-thousand feet at a speed of eight knots.

Admiral Lee then signaled for formation *Echelon Right.* That formation placed USS Indiana at the lead of a line of battleships at a forty-five-degree angle. This formation set each warship to the starboard and two-thousand feet to the rear of its predecessor. *Echelon Right or Left* is an aggressive formation, as it allows each battleship overlapping fields of fire against an opposing fleets line of battle. It is the precursor move to *Crossing the T*. Lee then ordered the formation *Line of Battle.* This maneuver would allow the naval formation to effectively cross the "T" of the enemy battle line.

Admiral McClintock, who shared the Bridge

with Admiral Lee and Flag Captain Powell congratulated Admiral Lee for the quickness and effectiveness of the maneuvers. Each battleship executed the plans with precision, maintaining their relative positions in the formations. Admiral Lee smiled then said: "Thank you, Admiral, it means a lot to hear that from a fellow professional." Then turning to Captain Powell, he said: "Signal fleet to form *Line Abreast* and increase speed to ten knots. Let's do this again." The formations were repeated a third time at twelve knots. All three attempts were considered to be successful.

McClintock was very impressed, but also puzzled as to why he, a Royal Navy Admiral was provided such close examination of United States Naval Tactics. The privilege was particularly puzzling as twelve years earlier, both nations were at war and had fought against each other three times in the past 100-years.

On the voyage back to Rio, Admiral Lee explained to Mcclintock: "Our nations have more common interests than issues that separate us. There are far more reasons for cooperation than for conflict. We are witnessing exciting times. The days of sail-powered battleships pounding each other in a line of battle are over. We are writing a new book on naval tactics. These tactics will evolve as gunnery and armor improve. You are witnessing the current cutting edge. What happens in a year or decade is yet to be decided.

My colleague Admiral Treat is practicing other maneuvers on his way back to Samana Bay. Depending on what happens in Chimbote Bay, Admiral Kincaid may be able to test them out in naval combat. Our goal, with the invitation by the Peruvian government, is to establish a naval base there peacefully. The Chileans show very aggressive tendencies and may test our resolve. They have been very successful against the Bolivians and Peruvians on both land and sea. I am concerned they will try to test our mettle. If so, the consequences will be on their heads."

The next day in Rio was full of activity. Ship's captains prepared their vessels to leave. Various ambassadors submitted numerous requests for inspection tours of the United States Navy battleships. Most were impressed with their advanced designs.

Ambassador Hilliard made appointments to further the discussions. Accommodations were available for those nations wishing the contract the construction of the Massachusetts Class Battleships for their navies.

The Brazilian Admiralty advised Emperor Pedro II that the United States would construct battleships for the Brazilian Navy. Pedro II ordered them to begin negotiations for two of the warships.

The Argentine Ambassador Juan Carlos DeFilippo expressed interest in negotiations for the purchase of existing warships, and the construction of the modern battleships.

Ambassador Higgins, after consulting with Admiral Lee arranged for a goodwill visit to Buenos Aires.

Admiral Lee had informed him that the new Maine Class battleships would surpass the Massachusetts Class battleships in size, tonnage, armor, and weapons. The three Maine Class warships were nearing completion in shipyards in Norfolk, Philadelphia, and Brooklyn. Three of the hulls of the newer Connecticut Class Battleships were under construction in Boston, Samana Bay, and Mare Island. Other navy yards were competing for the contracts for the remaining three battleships. These would be the first battleships constructed of steel.

The trip to Rio was considered to be a smashing success. Both Brazil and Argentina had expressed interest in purchasing existing warships, and others were eager to have new battleships constructed. With the successful trip to Rio, the voyage to Buenos Aires had great potential. The next morning, Admiral Lee's fleet sailed out of Rio and set course for Buenos Aires.

Chapter 5

On April 2, following the inauguration of Rafael Nunez, the new President of Columbia greeted the new United States Ambassador, Isaiah James, General Grissom, and Admiral Treat. The new President congratulated Isaiah on his promotion to Ambassador and expressed appreciation to Admiral Treat for his timely intervention in Cartegena. He also thanked General Grissom for the United States role in the hostage release, and the suppression of the rebellion in Cartegena.

In a private meeting with President Nunez, Ambassador James indicated that the United States looked forward to productive relations with Columbia. He mentioned the potential of joint projects, including the construction of a canal through Columbia's northern province of Panama. The French already had a contract to build a sea-level canal, similar to the Suez Canal.

Ambassador James stressed the impracticability of such a plan, as beyond the coastal plain the interior of the area is dominated by a range of mountains. Those mountains and the heavy rains would doom the French plan to failure.

Nunez understood the engineering difficulties facing the French plan, which was approved by his predecessor. He stated: "Let's see what happens to the French project. If it fails, we can negotiate your proposal."

Following the inauguration, Admiral Treat, General Grissom, and a military escort returned to Cartegena. There they boarded USS Puritan, and the fleet steamed to Samana Bay. After debarking General Grissom and the Buffalo Soldiers, Admiral Treat saw to the re-provisioning of his warships. He then took a carriage to his quarters at the Base Commanders Residence. There his wife, Abigail Adams Treat, provided him with a sailor's welcome home.

Abigail was the great-granddaughter of Samuel Adams. Roberts mother Annabelle Treat, true to her promise held a garden party at Treat House to celebrate Roberts return to Chelsea following the conquest of Nova Scotia and New Brunswick. Eighteen-year-old Abigail, with blond hair and pale blue eyes, captivated Robert. Annabelle was delighted when the usually glib Robert stumbled over his words when talking to Abigail.

Abigail listened intently, smiled often, and laughed when Robert poked fun at himself. Their attraction to each other was instantaneous. Following a three-month courtship, Robert asked her father for permission to propose. On June 1, 1869, Robert and Abigail celebrated their marriage, followed by a honeymoon in Paris.

For the next three years, Robert and Abigail lived in Annapolis due to Roberts appointment as the Superintendent of the

United States Naval Academy. Robert received another sea command to fight in the Spanish and American War following the Arapiles Incident. Robert received his second Admirals Star following his naval victories in the Battle of San Juan Puerto Rico and Havana, Cuba.

Robert then became the commandant of the new Samana Bay Naval Base. Abigail joined him, and they celebrated the birth of Robert Jr. in 1875, and William Samuel in 1877. As commandant, Admiral Treat served for six years, expanding the base and patrolling the Caribbean.

The next day Admiral Treat received a telegraph message, reporting that his father collapsed and died of an apparent heart attack. Treat sent telegraphs to the Navy Department requesting leave, and to the Charlestown Navy yard informing the duty officer that he and his family would return to Chelsea. The next day after appointing General Grissom as temporary base commander, with Captain Decatur as adjutant, the Admiral and his family boarded USS Dispatch for the three-day trip to the Charleston Navy Yard.

Arriving at the Navy Yard, Admiral Treat and his family were immediately placed on a carriage to Treat House in Chelsea. As the coach pulled up, servants rushed down the stairs to gather up the luggage. Admiral Treat and Abigail walked up the stairs with Robert and William following behind.

His mother Annabelle and his grandmother Abigail met them in the front hall and ushered them into the parlor where the embalmed William Treat laid in his casket. Robert placed his hand on his father's shoulder who looked serene, almost as if he was sleeping. Abigail put her comforting hand on her husband's shoulder; then they picked up young Robert and William. Both boys began to sob as Robert solemnly closed the casket.

The pallbearers slid rods into the bottom of the casket, picked it up, and carried it down the stairs to the horse-drawn hearse, for the short distance to the Methodist Church. The Treat Family walked behind. Grandmother Abigail, aged 90 who refused to ride in a carriage and walked with the family. The church was full of friends including Vice Admiral William Richardson, the Commandant of the Charlestown Navy yard. Following the service, William Treat was laid to rest in the family plot alongside the church.

On the walk back to Treat House, Admiral William Richardson asked Robert to visit him in his office the following week. Robert agreed, and they established an appointment.

For the next days, the family reminisced about their father's vibrant life. Robert's older brother, William who assumed control of the shipping business, regaled them all with tales of their fathers privateering voyages. They all laughed when William recounted his father's joy when, after the war, Admiral Dalghren sold back the de-commissioned *USS Rambler* and *USS Winnisimmet* for one-hundred dollars each.

The following week, Robert put on his Admiral's uniform and with Abigail rode in one of the family carriages to the Navy Yard. There they enjoyed lunch with Admiral Richardson and his wife, Molly. Following the meal, the two admirals adjourned to Richardson's office.

There, after smoking cigars, Richardson revealed that he was retiring on July 4th. Richardson stated: "Robert, you have been at sea for almost ten years. Your courage and exploits in war are the stuff of legends. I wish I had one-half of your initiative. My job is open. A word from me, and it is yours. Talk it over with Abigail and let me know by Friday."

With that, the Admirals rejoined their wives in the parlor. Abigail looked over at Robert. He smiled, and her smile became radiant. He asked: "You heard"? She nodded. Robert looked at Admiral Richardson and said,” “Well, Bill, that is your answer.” Abigail hugged her husband and said: “Finally, we can establish a home of our own.”

Following several telegrams to the Navy Department, Admiral Treat received the authorizations he needed. He boarded USS Dispatch for his final voyage to Samana Bay. There he promoted Captain Stephen Decatur to Commodore and appointed him as Base Commander. General Grissom received his second star an became the Army Force Commander in the Caribbean. Following a commissioning ceremony, Commodore Stephen Decatur assumed command of the Naval Base in Samana Bay. During the past five years of Admiral Treats tenure, the base expanded into an active shipbuilding center. Commodore Decatur promised to expand base activities.

Following the ceremony, Admiral Treat ordered the packing of his and Abigail’s personal effects, then boarded USS Dispatch for meetings at the Department of the Navy in Washington DC. There, he was surprised to see Abigail. At a ceremony, he received his third star. From there they boarded a train to Boston.

Chapter 6

April 4, 1861

Chimbote, Bay

Kincaid met with his Captains. He began: "The flagship will lead the attack on Chimbote Bay. Accompanying will be *USS Winslow, USS Atlas, USS Sword,* and *USS Spector. USS Atlas* will engage *Huascar. USS Kearsarge* and *USS Winslow* will engage *Almiralte Cochrane. USS Sword* and *USS Spector* will engage the Chilean Corvettes."

Then addressing Captain John Dalton, commander of *USS Satyr,* Kincaid stated: "John, I appoint you as brevet Commodore of the off-shore squadron. *USS Satyr* and *USS Mercury* will protect the troopships. *USS Atlas and USS Pegasus* will perform picket duty and be on the lookout for *Blanco Encalada*. If sighted, the pickets are not to engage. Their mission is to draw her back to *USS Satyr* and *USS Mercury.* Once that is accomplished *USS Satyr,* and *USS Mercury* will engage *Blanco Encalada* while the sloops protect the troopships from any escorts accompanying *Blanco Encalada*.

Chilean Navy Fleet

Sister ships *Almiralte Cochrane* and *Blanco Encalada* were British built iron battery battleships. Both had three masts and bark-rigged for added propulsion while at sea. Battery battleships were a compromise between the broadside ironclads and a turret ship. The Royal Navy Admiralty was late to the idea of giving up sail power. Typical of settlements, it took from both the broadside and turret ships but satisfied the requirements of neither.

Her hull was riveted iron four and one-half inches thick. An additional armor belt protected from below the waterline to the main deck. This belt consisted of ten-inches of Teak wood, covered with another 4 and one-half inches of riveted iron. The

Teakwood provided a cushioning layer between the iron hull and armor plate.

Six inches of armor plate protected the external box style batteries located amidships on both sides the hull. The weapons contained three, nine-inch Armstrong rifled muzzle-loaded guns, a 20-pound cannon, a nine-pound cannon, and a machine gun. When firing from the broadside, these warships were formidable.

The main guns were on tracks which allowed them to fire eleven degrees towards the bow and the stern. However, their elevation was limited by the internal gun ports, and their effective range was five miles.

An armor-piercing (AP) shell, striking on the broadside, could penetrate up to ten inches of armor. An experienced crew averaged between two and one-half to four-minutes to reload the guns. The guns were pointed down using hydraulics, sponged out twice to remove all hot embers, then the powder and shells were rammed in separately. The hydraulics raised the gun barrel to the firing position, where the gun crew aimed and fired.

This design contrasted with the turreted Puritan Class Monitors. The twin twelve-inch gun turrets mounted bow and stern provided a 240-degree angle of fire, and when elevated at forty-five degrees had a range of twelve miles. Plunging rounds could penetrate up to ten inches of armor plate. At an elevation of fifteen degrees, and at a distance of five miles, an (AP) shell could penetrate fifteen inches of armor. The breach loaded guns could be fired twice per minute.

Blanco Encalada was the flagship of Commodore Oscar Viel-Toro. She and three twenty-gun corvettes were in a hidden anchorage ten miles south of Chimbote Bay. This anchorage was almost invisible from the sea, looking like a river. The opening was a volcanic canal created when the roof of a lava tunnel from an extinct volcano collapsed. The crater had also collapsed, creating a deep water sheltered anchorage. The influx and egress of the tide had eroded the porous lava rock, allowing for safe passage of ships. Foliage, growing in the fertile lava soil created natural camouflage obstructing the view of the anchorage. Initially, it was a pirate base, with the Corsairs preying on commercial shipping. The anchorage had been abandoned and forgotten for decades until accidentally discovered by the Chilean Navy.

Riders from Chimbote Bay alerted Commodore Viel of Admiral Kincaid's demand; and of the expected attack. The four ships were made ready to sortie out of the hidden anchorage to attack the United States Navy troopships, while the Chilean Navy and land-based artillery defended Chimbote Bay.

At 6 am with a setting full moon, Commodore Oscar Viel-Toro ordered *Blanco Encalada* and the three Corvettes to sortie out of the hidden anchorage to attack the United States Navy transports and their escorts. He was confident that the trap was sprung. His task was to close the door.

Chapter 7.

March 30, 1881.

At 9 am, the sun burned off the morning mist. Battle stations sounded throughout the fleet. Watertight doors were secured as the crews operated their battle stations. *USS Kearsarge* led the assault into Chimbote Bay with Admiral Kincaid's flag flying briskly from the yardarm. Following in the line of battle were *USS Winslow, USS Atlas, USS Sword,* and *USS Spector*.

When all the warships entered the bay, the Chilean shore batteries started firing from both the north and south banks. Waterspouts erupted around the fleet. Cannon shells struck *USS Kearsarge* twice, and *USS Atlas* once, but the rounds ricocheted off the sloped armor. Admiral Lee signaled that the forward turrets of *USS Kearsarge, Winslow, and Atlas* fire at the north bank, and the rear turrets fire on the south. The Parrot rifles on *USS Sword* to fire on the north bank, and *USS Spector* on the south. Puffs of smoke from the batteries gave away their positions. The combined cannonade quickly suppressed the shore batteries on both banks.

Three previously unsighted steam-powered torpedo boats, each armed with two torpedos sortied from behind the Chilean corvettes and charged at the United States warships. The six-inch-long guns on *USS Kearsarge, USS Winslow, and USS Atlas* combined to lay down an intense barrage at the torpedo boats. The frigates USS Spector and USS Sword added the weight of their fifteen gun broadsides of thirty-two-pound cannons.

The Chilean torpedo boats, in a line abreast formation, charged bravely into this maelstrom of exploding shells. Suddenly, two rounds struck the middle ship, which exploded in a ball of flame. The other two boats fired their torpedoes and turned to flee. A near miss blew below one of the torpedo boats, lifting it out of the water. The torpedo boat slammed into the water bow first and broke in half. The third boat escaped as Admiral Kincaid's fleet were frantically attempting to avoid the torpedos.

After the Chilean boats had launched their weapons, the lookout cried, "torpedos in the water." The Captains ordered the Helmsmen to turn the bows parallel to the torpedos paths. USS Atlas turned too late, and a torpedo struck at an oblique angle port side, forward of the Bridge then exploded.

Captain O'Bannon was on the flying bridge and was struck by shrapnel, which knocked him down. He crawled to the speaking tube, instructed damage control to the area, and ordered half-speed. The watertight doors held and limited the flooding to two compartments. The other three torpedoes missed. Admiral Kincaid requested Captain Mahan to assist USS Atlas, and the other warships to form the line of battle.

Captain Charles Condell de LaHaza seized

the confusion to order *Almiralte Cochrane. Huascar* and the two corvettes to attack. The damage to *USS Atlas* had evened the battleship odds to an even fight. With *USS Sword* aiding the stricken *USS Atlas, USS Spectre* would have to fight the two corvettes.

Admiral Kincaid signaled *USS Winslow* to target *Huascar, USS Spectre* to fire on the Corvettes at the opportunity, and ordered Captain Powell to target *Almiralte Cochrane*. Kincaid's fleet was approaching at an oblique angle. He ordered a turn to port to cross the Chilean "T." The twelve-inch turrets turned, aimed and fired. The range was three miles, and waterspouts straddled the Chilean battleships, which turned to starboard to bring *Almiralte Cochrane's* battery into play. The next US Navy salvo scored hits, two on *Almiralte Cochrane* and one on *Huascar*. Almiralte Cochrane's armor absorbed the hits. The twelve-inch shell penetrated Huascar's thinner armor then exploded, showering wood and metal splinters killing or wounding crew in that area. The Chilean warship guns were at their extreme range, and their salvos fell short. Captain LaHaza ordered his warships to turn to close the distance as his guns reloaded.

Captain Dewey fired his six Parrot Rifles at the first Corvette and altered course to maintain the distance, as the Parrot Rifles outranged the Chilean guns. He ordered the thirty-two-pound guns run out and loaded on both broadsides. The third salvo scored two hits on the targeted corvette causing significant damage. Dewey ordered the Parrot Rifles to switch target to the second corvette, then turned to close on the first to bring his thirty-two-pound broadside into action. The Parrot Rifles turned on their tracks aimed and fired at the second warship.

Captain Mahon boarded *USS Atlas* to ascertain her condition. He learned that Captain O'Bannon was dead, and the executive officer Lt. Commander Connors was in command. After surveying the torpedo damage, Mahon determined that *USS Atlas* was not in danger of sinking and could defend itself. He re-boarded *USS Sword* and rejoined the fight.

The third Chilean torpedo boat re-armed and began an attack run, focusing on *USS Atlas*. *USS Sword* moved to intercept as the six-inch guns of *USS Atlas* began to fire. The Parrot Rifles on *USS Sword* fired as well as the thirty-two-pound broadside. The torpedo boat had to maintain a straight course to fire its torpedoes. The predictable path allowed for focused fire, with near misses and exploding shells churning up the water making aiming difficult. At extreme range, the Chilean Captain fired his two torpedos. Seconds later several rounds hit the torpedo boat which disintegrated in a ball of flame.

Lookouts on USS Atlas shouted "torpedos in the water." The helmsman turned the wheel sharply to port, but at five knots, the battleship responded slowly. The three Gatling guns fired at the torpedos, churning up the water in front of them. At one-hundred yards out the forward torpedo exploded. The shock wave caused the second torpedo to broach, diverting its course to the left. *USS Atlas* was turning hard to port. The weapon missed less than three feet to starboard.

As *USS Spectre* closed on the Chilean corvette, Captain Dewey ordered the gun captains to “fire as you bear.” One by one the port side15 thirty-two-pounders blasted their adversary at close range. When the broadside was completed, the corvette was a wreck. One mast was down, and dozens of crew members were dead or wounded. Dewey then ordered the helmsman to steer *USS Spectre* across the stern of the corvette and ordered another broadside into the unprotected stern. Once completed, the corvette was a de-masted hulk, listing to starboard. Satisfied that she was no longer a threat, Dewey ordered *USS Spectre* to close on the second corvette. The gun captains ran out the full fifteen starboard side thirty-two-pounders, and the gun crews stood at the ready.

The Chilean Captain tried to cross *USS Spectre's* stern. Dewey, anticipating the maneuver ordered the helmsman to turn hard to starboard, which countered the Chilean plan. The warships began to circle each other looking for an opportunity.

During these maneuvers, *USS Spectre's* Parrot rifles pounded the corvette. An explosive shot hit the corvette at the base of the Quarter Deck, with shrapnel killing the helmsman, allowing the wheel to spin out of control and knocking the Captain to the deck. Moments later, the corvette turned against the wind, which caused the sails to go slack. Dewey seized the opportunity, and *USS Spectre* came alongside the corvette and fired a broadside, which wreaked havoc from stem to stern. The foremast fell over the side, acting as an anchor. Realizing his battle was over, the Chilian Captain hauled down his flag.

USS Kearsarge targeted *Almiralte*

Cochrane, and USS Winslow focused *Huascar* with their twelve-inch guns, scoring additional hits on the charging Chilean warships. At two miles separation, the Chilean ships turned to bring all their weapons into play.

Almiralte Cochrane's three nine-inch battery fired with two near misses and one hit, which ricocheted off the sloping armor. *USS Kearsarge* replied with a salvo including the four twelve-inch guns and the three six-inch secondary weapons, achieving three hits. While the Chilean gun crews were re-loading their muzzle-loaded cannons, Kearsarge fired three more salvos, scoring four strikes.

USS Winslow also fired four salvos during the same time that Huascar shot two. The damage to Huascar was enormous with the forward turret knocked out of action with a direct hit at the base of the turret, jamming the mechanism. *Huascar* scored one hit which exploded on the side armor but did not penetrate. *USS Winslow* fired another salvo, tallying three hits near the waterline causing Huascar to list to starboard. With her main deck now exposed Huascar tried to turn away. *USS Winslow* fired another salvo, three shells penetrated the main deck, exploding inside *Huascar.* Smoke, then flames billowed out, then *Huascar* blew up.

USS Winslow then rotated the twelve-inch gun turrets to target *Almiralte Cochrane*. Both United States battleships fired salvos scoring a combined six hits, and knocking out two of the nine-inch Armstrong guns. Witnessing the destruction of *Huascar*, and the defeat of his corvettes, Captain Charles Condell de LaHaza hauled down his flag in surrender.

With the battle in Chimbote Bay won, Admiral Kincaid focused his binoculars on the troopship convoy. He saw smoke and heard the distant rumble of gunfire. He signaled *USS Winslow* to accept the surrender of *Almiralte Cochrane*, and Captain Mahon to escort *USS Atlas* towards the harbor dock. The two corvettes were dismasted hulks, slowly sinking, with their crews abandoning ship. Captain Dewey steamed towards the sinking warships and lowered lifeboats to assist in the rescue of the Chilean sailors. Admiral Kincaid then ordered Captain Powell to make full steam towards the troop convoy.

Chapter 8.

Commodore Oscar Viel-Toro on the quarterdeck of the battleship *Blanco Encalada* positioned his three corvettes in a crescent-shaped screen two miles ahead. The main-top lookout shouted: "Signal from *El Conde enemy in sight, a sloop of war bearing five degrees north-northeast, distance five-miles."* Viel-Toro ordered his flag captain to battle-stations, and full speed ahead." *Blanco Encalada* surged forward to catch up with her consorts.

Minutes later the main-top lookout shouted: "*Signal from El Conde, the second sloop of war is sighted. Permission to engage."* Viel-Toro glanced at his flag captain and nodded. The flag captain then said: "*Signal to El Conde – engage as you are able*." The three Chilean corvettes beat to quarters and powered up the steam engines to close the distance.

The main-top lookout on *USS Atlas* shouted

"*Enemy in sight, three corvettes distance four miles 350 degrees west-southwest.* Minutes later the lookout shouted: "Battleship sighted, the same bearing distance of five miles." USS Atlas relayed the signals to USS Pegasus. With signal flags flying, both warships came about to comply with Commodore Dalton's orders.

USS Satyr's masthead lookout reported the signals to Commodore Dalton. He signaled *USS Mercury* to engage the corvettes, *USS Pegasus* and *USS Atlas* to fall back to protect the troopships, and that *USS Satyr* would engage *Blanco Encalada*. All the ships captains acknowledged the orders. Commodore Dalton ordered full speed ahead.

Commodore Oscar Viel-Toro observed the pending order of battle. He was confident that *Blanco Encalada* could defeat the United States Navy battleship and that his three corvettes could severely damage the other battleship. After beating his opposing battleship, he could finish off the other.

Then the troopship convoy would be his. He did not know the progress of the battle in Chimbote Bay but could hear heavy cannon fire. He was confident in the abilities of Captain Charles Condell de LaHaza and the defenses he had established along the shore.

When the rangefinder on *USS Satyr* indicated seven miles, Commodore Dalton ordered the forward turret to fire a ranging shot. Several seconds later a waterspout erupted one-quarter mile short of the approaching *Blanco Encalada.* Dalton ordered a quarter turn to starboard and for the second gun to fire. That shell impacted 100 yards short. Dalton then ordered both turrets to fire a salvo. The four shells straddled *Blanco Encalada.*

Viel-Toro, realizing he had to close the distance to bring his guns to bear ordered more steam, The captain protested that the boiler was already at 100 percent. Viel-Toro glared at him then said: "Our destruction will be assured before we can fire if we don't close the range. More steam, now!" The captain told the chief engineer to release the safeties on the boiler. Within a minute, *Blanco Encalada* surged forward.

Commodore Dalton ordered continuous fire, with the elevation of the guns decreasing with each salvo. The first hit struck *Blanco Encalada* on the deck behind the bow, penetrated then exploded, showering wood and metal splinters, with eight crew members killed. The second hit struck the armor on the forward side of the starboard battery then blew up. The ironclad held, with minimal damage.

Two more shells hit seconds later on the main deck. One exploded on impact, the other penetrated before exploding. A dozen more crew were down, and *Blanco Encalada* still was out of range of her guns. Viel-Toro stomped his feet in frustration as he paced around the quarter-deck. Another shell exploded above the quarter-deck, killing the captain. Viel-Toro screamed his frustration at the Chief Engineer who approached indicating the boilers could not hold much more pressure. “More speed” was all he could shout. Finally, at four miles from his adversary, Viel-Toro ordered the helmsman to turn hard to port. The battery of Armstrong rifled muzzleloaders fired. Waterspouts erupted alongside *USS Satyr*.

Commodore Dalton ordered a full broadside fired, including the three, six-inch casement mounted rifled breech loaders. Waterspouts straddled *Blanco Encalada,* with three hits on her armor plate. The explosions peeled away armor but did not penetrate. It was now a slugging match between two battleships. Dalton ordered a course change to cut across the bow of *Blanco Encalada.* Viel-Toro countered to maintain the broadside battle. Both warships pounded each other, with the armor repelling most hits. Slowly, USS Satyr, with its more rapid rate of fire and sloped armor gained the advantage as damage began to mount on *Blanco Encalada*.

USS Mercury steered a course to bring it between the corvettes. The forward twelve-inch battery focused on a corvette on the left, the rear turret on the warship on the right. The three six-inch casement guns fired broadsides from both sides. The corvettes returned fire with their seven and nine-inch Armstrong guns. However, the shells ricocheted off the sloped armor plate. One by one, *USS Mercury's* gunfire sank the corvettes.

The third corvette made a run at the troopships, but *USS Atlas and USS Pegasus* intercepted her before she could get into range. Both *Atlas* and *Pegasus* fired their three fifteen-inch Parrot rifles at the corvette, scoring several hits. The Chilean warship fought back bravely, hitting both *Atlas* and *Pegasus*. However, she sank within thirty minutes of the start of the battle.

USS Mercury steamed to aid *USS Satyr* in the fight against *Blanco Encalada.* The broadsides from both *Satyr* and *Mercury* stripped away the armor protecting *Blanco Encalada.* Two shells struck the quarter-deck killing Viel-Toro and the helmsman. With significant gaps in the armor protection, rounds penetrated the gun batteries, exploding and killing most of the gun crews.

The end came when the steam pressure exceeded the boiler's capacity, which ruptured and exploded with flames erupting through the main deck. Surviving crew members began jumping overboard. Within minutes *Blanco Encalada* rolled over and sank.

USS Satyr and USS Mercury lowered boats to rescue surviving Chilean sailors. During this rescue mission, *USS Kearsarge* arrived on the scene. Gratified to observe that all his warships were intact, Admiral Kincaid signaled the fleet to follow him into Chimbote Bay. Seeing that the United States Navy had defeated the Chilean naval forces, the Chilean ground commander Colonel Aquino asked for terms. Kincaid informed him that his soldiers would have to stack their weapons and board a troopship for repatriation to Chile. The officers could keep their swords and sidearms. Aquino agreed and together with the surviving Chilean sailors boarded two troop ships for the return to Chile.

United States Marines debarked from the troopships and occupied the former Chilean barracks. Salvage operations began on the sunken Chilean warships. Kincaid assigned Captain Dewey as commander of USS Atlas. With her damage repaired and escorted by USS Sword, USS Atlas sailed to San Francisco for permanent repairs with Admiral Kincaid's full report of the battle and its aftermath.

The Almiralte Cochrane was repaired and presented to the Peruvian Navy. Two weeks later, Peruvian sailors boarded the warship and took custody of the vessel. Steamships brought Peruvian workers to assist in the construction of the United States Naval Base.

In the months following the battle, Peruvian troops regained the initiative over the Chilean occupying forces. The Chilean army, which briefly occupied Lima, suffered from the lack of naval logistical supplies and support. The Peruvians, on the other hand, were provided with modern weapons and logistical support from the United States.

The Peruvian Navy used the Almiralte Cochrane to bombard Chilean seaports and intercept supply convoys. During a raid on Valparaiso, the Almiralte Cochrane sank following an attack by Chilean torpedo boats.

Suffering from shortages of arms and ammunition, the Chilean Army retreated, surrendering up most of their Peruvian conquered territory. The war dragged on for two more years. Great Britain, alarmed by the growing United States hegemony in South America, and the German Empire's provision to the Chileans of armaments and logistical support; offered to act as a mediator to end the war.

Peru, Bolivia, and Chile were exhausted, and an armistice was declared. The peace treaty signed on October 20, 1883, shifted the previously undefined and disputed boundaries. Peru regained its lost territories except for its southernmost province of Tarapeca which went to Chile. Bolivia became landlocked as Chile conquered the coastal region of Antofagasta and its only seaport.

Peru considered the outcome to be a victory due to its alliance with the United States. That alliance brought a thriving seaport to Chimbote Bay, with railroad and telegraph connections to Lima. Peru also made arrangements for the purchase of the ironclads USS Monadnock and the converted USS Deli from the United States.

The United States Navy constructed a significant naval base at Chimbote Bay, adjacent to the seaport. A second city was under construction to house naval support personnel and the families of the sailors. The United States Department of the Navy administered the naval base. Within months schools were established, and the local economy began to thrive. The hidden inlet used by the Chilean Navy became a tourist destination. The Peruvians cleared the land and constructed hotels and restaurants to serve the growing tourist trade.

Chile gained two provinces, including the significant discoveries of nitrate and guano located in Antofagasta. Chilean civilian migration into its new territories increased to take advantage of these new resources. The war also pushed Chile into the orbit of the United Kingdom, which agreed to construct two fast cruisers for the Chilean Navy. Chile then ordered a new modern battleship.

Upon their arrival at the Mare Island Naval Base, Captain's Dewey and Alfred Thayer Mahn received hero welcomes. Naval Command confirmed Dewey as Captain of

USS Atlas, and Captain Mahn received a prestigious appointment as a professor at the Naval War College. There, he earned acclaim for his advanced theories on naval tactics. The Navy also sent a dispatch ship to Chimbote Bay confirming Captain Dalton's appointment to Commodore and awarded Admiral Kincaid with a second star. Commodore Dalton was ordered home for re-assignment as Commodore of a new fast cruiser squadron.

The successful campaigns in Columbia and Chimbote; and the successful diplomatic missions to Brazil and Argentina reinforced the prestige and hegemony of the United States in South America. Internationally, with the affirmation of The Monroe Doctrine, South America became recognized to be within the United States sphere of influence.

Chapter 9.

October 15, 1881.

Berlin, German Empire.

At the suggestion of the United States, the European powers scheduled an international conference involving the colonialization of Africa. Up to that time, The German Empire did not have any African Colonies. Therefore, Berlin was considered to be a neutral Capitol. Attending countries included: Austria Hungary, Belgium, Denmark, France, The German Empire, Italy, Netherlands, The Ottoman Empire, Portugal, Russia, Spain, Sweden-Norway, The United Kingdom and the United States. With the conference situated in Berlin, the delegates elected Chancellor Otto Von Bismark as the chairman.

Each nation sent a Plenipotentiary to the conference. Secretary of State Garfield represented the United States. Garfield was the guest of Admiral Lee and arrived in Hamburg in an impressive convoy, escorted by the Battleships USS Indiana and USS Massachusetts. Admiral Lee made an initial stop in Monrovia, Liberia. There the Liberian delegation joined the entourage.

Liberia, while not being explicitly invited to the conference, assigned General Obadiah Driver as a Liberian delegate to the United States delegation. He had full Plenipotentiary authority. Accompanying him was his young wife Amelia, who was the niece of President Taylor. In Hamburg, General Driver arrived in his dress uniform with enough medals to rival any of the European minor prince's regalia.

Up to this point, the European powers had colonized areas bordering the oceans. With the discovery of substantial natural resources, expansion into the interior became a paramount concern. Boundary disputes were inevitable, and conflicts could lead to war. The powers, following much debate, developed the Doctrine of Effective Occupation.

The principle stated that powers could acquire rights over colonial lands only if they possessed them or had "effective occupation." In other words, if they had treaties with local leaders, if they flew their flag there, and if they established an administration in the territory to govern it, with a police force to keep order. The colonial power could also make use of the colony economically. This principle became famous not only as a basis for the European powers to acquire territorial sovereignty in Africa but also could be used to settle boundary disputes.

Liberia satisfied the Principle of Effective Occupation along the border of Ivory Coast up the Milo River to the Niger River. They had colonized the area, established military outposts, and had a sufficient police force. The territory between there and the Sierra Leone boundary was ill-defined. All concerned parties agreed to an arbitrary line drawn from the Niger River to the Sierre Leone town of Koidu. The south side of the line was confirmed to be part of Liberia.

Under a separate agreement between the United Kingdom and France, the northern border was determined to be under the French sphere of influence. General Driver was satisfied as for the first time, all the European Powers recognized Liberia's existence, and defined its borders.

With the Liberian issue settled, the United States delegation withdrew from the conference. Secretary Garfield reassured the European powers that with the new Liberian boundaries recognized, the United States had no further interest in Africa. Furthermore, he stated that the United States would not bind itself to any other agreements decided by the conference.

Following a weeks journey, the United States Navy convoy reached Monrovia. General Driver and Amelia were guests on the bridge of USS Indiana when they steamed into Monrovia. Obadiah was delighted to observe another convoy of cargo ships unloading building materials and long guns to reinforce Monrovia's protection from Forts Monroe and Clay.

The next day, President Taylor hosted a celebratory reception at the presidential mansion. Disclosure of the full details of the border settlement delighted the guests. An international crisis was averted, and for the first time, Liberia's boundaries were internationally recognized.

With diamond wealth flooding the treasury, President Taylor was eager to upgrade his military. An order was presented to purchase a new Massachusetts Class battleship, and two of the new class of fast cruisers. The cruisers were capable of speeds more than twenty knots. Liberia's mercantile fleet was growing, and so was the threat of piracy. The cruiser class warships were required to interdict the pirates or hunt them down once they attacked.

As the Canonicus Class monitors were aging, Taylor also ordered two Puritan Class Monitors for coastal defense. With the delivery the Puritan Class Monitors, the Canonicus Monitors would serve as river patrol.

General Driver was eager to learn about the new upgrades to the Gatling guns. He also placed a large order for Spencer repeating rifles and ammunition. These weapons would enhance the protection provided by the garrisons in the new territory.

Chapter 10

September 5, 1883.

Halifax, Nova Scotia, and Fredericton, New Brunswick

General elections occurred across these territories. The issues were to apply for statehood or to remain as territories. For the previous ten years, municipal elections selected mayors, city councils, and representatives to each of the territory assemblies. The President appointed the territorial governors. The territories elected non-voting representatives to Congress. The sentiment was supportive of full statehood.

The population in both territories almost doubled since their acquisition by the United States. Some of the increase came from mostly Irish foreign immigration, but mostly the migration came from New Englanders looking for greener pastures. These new residents pressured the territorial legislatures to press for statehood. One week later, the final vote count indicated that over 75% of the ballots cast were for statehood. New elections were scheduled for November to elect governors, state representatives and senators, and federal representatives.

On December 3, 1883, by acclamation, the United States 47th Congress admitted New Brunswick and Nova Scotia as States in the United States of America. In the November elections, Nova Scotia elected three Representatives, and New Brunswick chose two. The Parti Patriote dominated at the polls.

The newly elected State Senate chambers met to elect two Senators. With the Parti Patriote dominant, the state sent an entire Parti-Patriot delegation to Washington. The new Representatives and Senators were administered their oaths of office and took their seats.

The Union now totaled forty-three states, including four formerly in Canada. The representatives and senators from these states formed a caucus to coordinate common interests. That caucus was a mixture of Republicans, Democrats and Parti Patriote members. They realized they had more of common interest together than political party interests allowed. Voting as a block, they could be instrumental in affecting legislation. As individual party members, their capability to influence change was limited.

Republican and Democrat Party leaders took note and made efforts to discipline their members. That effort pushed the caucus members into a closer relationship and engendered objections from the membership who felt their independence also threatened. Fearing that too much pressure applied to a small internal revolt, could lead to a new political party, the leadership backed off. The new caucus grew in political power and began to attract support, particularly on issues which crossed over congressional districts.

November 5, 1984.

President Blaine narrowly won re-election over his Democrat opponent Grover Cleveland. His margin of victory was less than 50,000 votes. The Republicans regained control of the Senate. However, the Democrats retained control of the House of Representatives.

May 1, 1885.

Encouraged by events in Nova Scotia and New Brunswick, voters went to the polls in Cuba and Puerto Rico. The issues were the same. There were two questions on the ballot. The first one was a vote for statehood. The second was to remain as territories. A simple YES or NO would decide the issues. In Puerto Rico, statehood won 70 percent of the vote. In Cuba, statehood was victorious with an 80 percent majority.

Two weeks later, in a pre-existing special session, Congress voted to accept the applications for statehood. Primary elections occurred on July 1, to elect district legislatures and senators, and candidates for Congressional districts. Based on the 1880 census, Puerto Rico would have three congressional districts, while Cuba would have seven. Run-off elections held in September narrowed the field to one Republican and one Democrat in each district.

Significant numbers of southern blacks moved to both Cuba and Puerto Rico. Those voters tipped the scales in the November elections. Republicans won five of Cuba's seven congressional districts, and two of the three in Puerto Rico. More significantly, the Republicans won control of both of the State Senate chambers. That resulted in the selection of four Republican Senators increasing Republican majority to six seats. That election also reduced the Democrat control in the House of

Representatives to twelve positions.

The United States Congress and Senate exhibited more diversity than ever. Conversely, it also became more sectarian. Regional alliances were developing focusing on common ground within the various caucuses. The Democrat and Republican Parties leadership teams encountered increasing difficulties to mold working coalitions.

Following the example of the four formerly Canadian States, the Caribbean States senators and representatives from Cuba, Dominica, and Puerto Rico allied in a caucus devoted to their unique issues. Their population was evolving into a distinctly "creole" mix of black, Hispanic and white. The three states enjoyed prosperous and growing economies with industries moving there to take advantage of warm summers and mild winters. Tourist resorts rivaled Florida in efforts to attract northern visitors.

The chemical pesticide DDT, developed in 1874 by an Austrian chemist Othmar Zeidler, was attributed to the rapid industrial expansion in the Carribean States. Zeidler did not know how to use the chemical and was unable to create a market. Zeidler's son Johann, also a chemist moved to the United States. Johann set up a chemical company to market his products and purchased the patent for DDT which is an organic colorless, tasteless and almost odorless crystalline solid. He brought a quantity of DDT with him to determine if he could find and develop a market.

While visiting the American Naval Base at Hamilton, Bermuda; he met with physicians treating Yellow Fever, Typhus, and Malaria. The physicians despaired of finding a cure. Johann noted flies and mosquitos everywhere tormenting the sick soldiers. Johann accidentally spilled a small amount of DDT into drainage water contaminated with flies. All the flies and mosquitos were dead the next day. Johann experimented with other drainage ditches and discovered the same result. He offered to spray his mix in the hospital wards and grounds to make the soldiers more comfortable. The flies and mosquitos were killed or driven off. Soon the recovery rate of the soldiers began to improve. At that moment, Johann knew he had found his market.

The United States Department of Defense purchased large quantities of the pesticide to apply in a powdered form or mix with water and spray in and around their military bases, located in hot and humid climates where Yellow Fever, Typhus, and Malaria were prevalent. Within two years, cases of the three diseases dropped by two-thirds. Private industry in these areas also purchased the chemical and spraying became widespread. Over the next five years, new cases became increasingly rare and less severe.

Bermuda and the Bahamas lagged in population growth. Mainly this happened due to poor soil, resulting in unsuccessful efforts in agriculture. The islands were unable to sustain their population and became dependent on the United States Navy and Army for financial support. Both island groups became territories, ruled by appointed military governors.

Elections 1888 to 1894.

The Presidential Elections were a rematch of 1884. However, Grover Cleveland won the Presidency by 20,000 votes. Blaine's support from Irish immigrants evaporated when a prominent Protestant Minister equated the Democrats as a "Party of Rum, Romanism, and Rebellion." Exhibiting the disenfranchisement with the national parties, the Republicans won 25 seats in the House of Representatives and enjoyed a majority of 199 – 157. In the Senate, the Republicans held the majority by 50 – 40.

The United States admitted four more states, Montana, North Dakota, South Dakota, and Washington in 1889. Idaho and Wyoming followed in 1890. Special elections held in those stated elected seven more Republicans to the House of Representatives. The State Senate selected three Democrats and three Republicans. These elections solidified Republican control of Congress.

In 1892, Cleveland easily won reelection, and the Democrats gained 23 House seats, the Populists won 3. The Democrats regained control of the House. Thirteen days before Cleveland's second inauguration disaster struck the Democrats.

It began with the collapse of global commodity prices as the result of crop failures in Argentina. Then the Reading and Philadelphia Railroads became insolvent. There was a run on gold and the banks. United States unemployment rose from 4 percent in 1890 to 18.4 percent in 1894. In the elections of 1894, the Democrats lost 130 seats. A worldwide depression was in full force.

Chapter 11.

The 1890s were a tumultuous decade for the United States of America. On January 20, 1891, The Hawaiian King Kalakaua died of Brights Disease in San Francisco while touring California. The Cruiser *USS Charleston* returned his body to Hawaii on January 29. His sister and Heir Apparent, Lili'uokalani, ascended to the throne. A controversy resulted when she tried to change the Constitution of 1887, which was highly favorable to large landowners and disenfranchised many native Hawaiians.

Queen Lili'uokalani toured the islands, speaking on behalf of a new Constitution to replace the 1887 document. She received overwhelming support from the people, but when she presented it to her Cabinet, they refused, as it was likely to lead to the overthrow of the government.

In January 1893, members of the American

Committee of Safety led a coup to overthrow Queen Lili'uokalani. A brief standoff took place between 500 Royal Guards and 1,500 members of the Hawaiian Rifles. This militia was a mix of European and United States citizens, who were also subjects of the Queen.

Alarmed for the safety of United States citizens and property, the Committee of Safety appealed to United States Minister Stevens to intervene. Stevens ordered the captain of the cruiser *USS Boston* to dispatch a company of United States Marines and a company of armed sailors to protect the grounds of the United States Embassy. Unwilling to face conflict with the Marines and sailors, the Royal Guards confined themselves to their barracks.

Without any opposition, the Committee for Safety overthrew the Queen and replaced her with the provisional government. Sanford B Dole was named the President of the Provisional Government of Hawaii. The new republic was recognized within 48 hours by all nations with diplomatic ties to the Kingdom of Hawaii, including the United States and the United Kingdom.

President Cleveland commissioned the Blount Report, which after an investigation called the overthrow of the monarchy illegal, and accused Minister Stevens and the United States Military of complicity in the Coup. Cleveland then issued a demand for the Queen's restoration.

President Cleveland appointed Albert Willis to be Minister to Hawaii. Willis was sent to Hawaii on a secret mission to meet with deposed Queen Liliʻuokalani and obtain a promise of amnesty for those involved in the overthrow of the monarchy; if Cleveland restored her to the throne. Willis reported to the Secretary of State in Washington that the deposed Queen was intent on killing the culprits. There was a dispute on terminology. Willis reported the Queen said "beheading"; Liliʻuokalani later said she used the word "execute."

Finally, the Queen reversed herself and told Willis she could issue an amnesty. On December 18, 1893, Willis demanded on behalf of Cleveland that the Committee for Safety dissolve the Provisional Government of Hawaii and to restore the Queen to power. Willis' mission was a failure when President Dole sent a written reply declining the surrender of his authority to the deposed queen.

President Cleveland then referred the matter to Congress, which commissioned the Morgan Report which exonerated the U.S. Minister and peacekeepers from taking any part in the Hawaiian Revolution. Following the Morgan Report, Cleveland reversed his stance, rebuffed the Queen's further pleas for interference, and maintained normal diplomatic relations with Provisional Government.

Following the approval of a new Constitution, the Provisional Government of

Hawaii ended on July 4, 1894. Sanford B Dole became President of the Republic of Hawaii. Willis remained as Ambassador to the Republic of Hawaii until his death on January 6, 1897. After an elaborate State Funeral at the Iolani Palace, the United States returned Willis's body to Kentucky for burial.

1896 Elections:

The worldwide depression deepened in 1895. President Cleveland was unable to reverse the downturn in the United States economy. The Populist Party was growing, taking Democratic voters into their ranks, particularly in the farm states where many farmers and ranchers were in danger of defaulting on their mortgages. In early 1896, the economy began to turn for the better. As manufacturing began to increase, thousands of factory workers returned to work.

William McKinley, the Governor of Ohio, easily won the Republican nomination. The convention then nominated Garret Hobart from New Jersey as Vice President. The maintenance of the Gold Standard was the key plank on Republican Party Platform. McKinley campaigned from his front porch entertaining delegations of Republicans and industrialists. Surrogates did the campaigning across the country.

Severely divided, the Democrats entered their convention, with no clear front-runner. The party leaders split almost evenly over the currency issue. Nearly one-half favored the Gold Standard, with the balance supporting free silver.

The 36-year old congressman from Nebraska, William Jennings Bryan delivered the Key Note Address. He eloquently advocated for free silver. He ended his speech by passionately spreading his arms as he exclaimed: "*You shall not press down upon the brow of labor this crown of thorns, you shall not crucify mankind upon a cross of gold.*" The speech so electrified the convention that the delegates nominated

Bryan as their candidate for president. Bryan was only 36 years old, and his experience as an officeholder was limited to two terms in the House of Representatives.

The Populists, seeing their major issue co-opted also nominated Bryan, as did the Free Silver Party. The Populists in an attempt to retain their identity nominated Thomas Watson as Vice President. Unlike McKinley, Bryan barnstormed across the United States with his idea of a devalued United States Dollar. His plan was for 16 Silver dollars for every gold dollar.

On November 3, seventy-nine percent of the voters went to the polls. McKinley won resoundingly by almost one-million votes with a smashing Electoral College victory of 319 – 177.

The Congressional elections were somewhat different. The Republicans lost 44 seats; thirty-one of which were in traditional Democrat districts, and went to the Republicans in the previous election in

1894. The Populists won 13 seats in the same manner. The Parti Patriote retained their five seats, and the Free Silver Party retained their one member. The final total included 230 Republicans, 124 Democrats, 22 populists, 5 Parti Patriote, and 1 Free silver. Following the election, the Populist Party slowly disappeared, with their members being absorbed by the Democrats. However, Populist principles dominated the Democrat Party for the next twenty years.

On March 4, 1897, William McKinley celebrated his inauguration as President of the United States. Attending one of his inauguration parties, the President of Hawaii Sanford Dole proposed a meeting to discuss common interests. McKinley instructed Secretary of State John Sherman to set up the meeting. One week later, President McKinley hosted Samuel Dole at the White House.

Following an exchange of pleasantries, Dole brought up the salient point for the meeting.

"Mr. President, my Privy Council has authorized me to either establish a formal alliance between the Republic of Hawaii and the United States or seek the annexation of the Republic into the United States. Our overall goal is to become part of the United States, but if a formal alliance is a prerequisite, we will seek that first."

McKinley was delighted at the potential of annexation. In a famous quotation, McKinley said: "We need Hawaii just as much and a good deal more than we did California. It is Manifest Destiny." Realizing the acquisition would have to be a step by step process, McKinley sent Secretary of State John Sherman to Hawaii negotiate a formal alliance. Sherman returned in June with the treaty. One of the provisions was a 99-year lease for to the exclusive military use of Pearl Harbor. The commercial harbor was open to shipping traffic of all nations. The treaty was submitted to the Senate for approval and passed with only ten dissenting votes. McKinley had expressed expansionist fervor in the campaign. His attitude differed with Cleveland's more isolationist disposition. Cleveland favored the construction of fast cruisers over battleships to protect the United States shipping interests. The development of naval battleships had languished after the completion of the three warships in the Maine Class, and the *USS Connecticut* touted as the first of a new generation of battleships.

McKinley, before being elected, attended a lecture given by Captain Alfred Thayer Mahan at the Naval War College. In his speech, Captain Mahan postulated: "*The primary mission of a navy was to secure the command of the sea, which would permit the maintenance of sea communications for one's ships while denying their use to the enemy and, if necessary, closely supervise neutral trade.*

Control of the sea could be achieved not by the destruction of commerce but only by destroying or neutralizing the enemy fleet. Such a strategy called for the concentration of naval forces composed of capital ships, not too large but numerous, well-manned with crews thoroughly trained, and operating under the principle that the best defense is an aggressive offense."

McKinley was very impressed with Captain Mahan's presentation. After winning the Presidency, he invited Captain Mahan to the White House to learn more. Mckinley also requested the attendance of his Secretary of the Navy, retired Admiral Robert Treat. Captain Mahan expressed awe to be in the presence of the President and the legendary admiral.

The *USS Connecticut* was the lead ship of her class of six large battleships. She was the only one currently commissioned. At Mahan's suggestion, and with the agreement of Secretary Treat, McKinley ordered the completion of the other five battleships.

On June 1, 1897, Secretary of the Navy Robert Treat gave the commencement speech at the Naval Academy Graduation and Commissioning Ceremony. Midshipman Robert Treat Jr. graduated fifth in his class and received his commission as Ensign; with a subsequent appointment to the USS Connecticut. His mother Abigail proudly watched from the reviewing stand as the graduating midshipmen marched past to take their seats located on the parade ground.

Within two years the six battleships were commissioned. They were the largest, and most heavily armed battleships in the United States Navy. McKinley, Secretary Treat, and Captain Mahan attended the naval review in the Chesapeake Bay. There *USS Connecticut* led her sister ships *USS Louisiana, USS Vermont, USS Kansas, USS Minnesota,* and *USS New Hampshire* in the review of the fleet. Each battleship measured 456 feet in length, 77 feet wide, and had the main armament of four, 12-inch guns in two turrets, one fore and the other aft. There were four twin turrets of 8-inch guns, also mounted fore and aft. There were twelve casements of 7-inch guns, six to each side. Combined these weapons constituted a significant broadside.

For close-in point defense, each side contained ten rapid-firing 3-inch guns and six fast-firing 2-inch guns. These guns were designed to combat lightly armored destroyers and torpedo boats. Each battleship also mounted four submerged torpedo tubes, two per side. The battlewagons. had a top speed of nineteen knots, which allowed them to maintain position with the fast cruisers.

On the drawing board was a revolutionary class of more massive big-gun battleships. These battleships would have four twelve-inch super-firing gun turrets. The casement guns would be for point defense and consist of 22 three-inch and ten one-inch rapid-firing guns. The first ship scheduled would be the *USS South Carolina*, with anticipated delivery in 1905.

Chapter 12

Pearl Harbor, Hawaii

On March 1, 1898, a courier ship sailed into Pearl Harbor with urgent dispatches for Admiral Kincaid. He was instructed to sail to Hong Kong to await developments in the Philippines. A significant revolt was in progress against Spanish rule.

Complicating the issue was the presence of the German Far East Fleet consisting of two armored cruisers and three fast cruisers. The German Empire was anxious to expand its empire in the Far East, and Spanish possessions looked to be lucrative easy acquisitions. The United States had numerous mercantile enterprises in the Philippines, which needed protection.

On March 4, Kincaid's fleet left Pearl Harbor. Kincaid's flagship, the Battleship *USS Connecticut* led the fleet out of the harbor. Other vessels following inline included: the Battleship *USS Missouri*, five cruisers: USS *Olympia, USS Baltimore, USS Boston, USS Charleston,* and USS *Raleigh;* two gunboats, USS *Concord* and USS *Petrel;* and the revenue cutter USS *McCulloch.* The fleet arrived in Hong Kong on March 25. There he learned that the mostly Filipino crew and some junior officers of the Spanish Navy mutinied, and were in control of the Spanish Pacific Squadron. Portions of Manila had fallen to the rebels. The rebels besieged the remnants of the Spanish Army at the fortress in Cavite.

The rebels also surrounded the American Consul, his diplomats, and surviving American merchants at the United States Consulate; protected by a platoon of United States Marines. In the confusion of the rebel advances, the Consul sent a dispatch to Hong Kong providing the most recent dispositions of rebel forces, and that the rebels mined the North Chanel, past Corregidor into Manila Bay.

Kincaid ordered the re-coaling of his warships and received permission from the US Consul General to purchase two freighters as supply ships the *SS Nanshan* and *SS Safiro.* These he loaded with food and munitions. On March 29, 1898, *USS Connecticut* led the United States Navy fleet out of Hong Kong. On their way out, they passed the German Empire's Far East Squadron arriving in port. Upon hearing the news about the Philippines, the German Admiral re-coaled his warships and headed towards Manila Bay.

Kincaid's fleet entered Subic Bay on April 3. Kincaid sent the revenue cutter *USS McCulloch* to investigate the cause of smoke on the horizon. Several hours later *USS McCulloch* returned with the news of the approaching German Fleet. Admiral Kincaid held a conference with his captains. He divided his fleet into two squadrons; and appointed Captain George Dewey to be Commodore of the Cruiser Squadron consisting of USS *Olympia, USS Baltimore, USS Boston, USS Charleston,* and USS

Raleigh. Dewey was instructed to enter Manila Bay by the South Channel. If fired upon by the Filipino warships, Dewey was ordered to engage and destroy. Admiral Kincaid and the remaining ships would establish a blockade of Subic Bay.

Dewey's flagship, the *USS Olympia*, was commanded by Captain Charles V. Gridley, who was the next most senior captain and transferred over from *USS Charleston.* At midnight, Commodore Dewey entered Manila Bay through the South Channel.

The Filipino warships, mostly obsolete cruisers sallied out to meet Dewey's flotilla. Dewey standing on the Bridge spoke to Captain Gridley: "You may fire when ready Gridley." Olympia's eight-inch guns fired, followed by the other cruiser's guns. Within an hour, the Filipino Navy warships including *Tina Castina, Castilla, Isla de Luzon, isle de Cuba, and Velasco* were burning wrecks that grounded themselves on shoals to prevent sinking.

During the sea battle, the Filipino ground forces assaulted the defenders at the fortifications at Cavite. Following hard hand to hand fighting, the Spanish drove off the attackers. Dewey then ordered two companies of Marines ashore to link up with the Consulate. Undercover of a naval bombardment, the Marines lifted the siege.

USS McCulloch steamed into the bay to obtain a status update. She passed the wrecked and burned Filipino warships. Commodore Dewey signaled that the Marines secured the consulate, and it was safe to bring in the supply ships through the South Chanel.

Admiral Kincaid hoisted the parlay flag as the German East Asia Squadron Subic Bay at 8 am. The German commander Rear Admiral Otto Von Diederichs accepted the invitation to board *USS Connecticut*. With the sound of distant gunfire as a background, the stewards served coffee and sweet bread to the admirals as they engaged in a courteous exchange of views.

Von Diederichs offered assistance. Kincaid was adamant that the engagement was entirely an American effort, and support by the German Empire was not needed. He offered Von Diederichs a tour of *USS Connecticut* which was accepted.

As the Admirals chatted amicably on the bridge wing, USS McCulloch steamed into view with signal flags flying. Dewey read the signals and said to Von Diederichs: "The Filipino Navy no longer exists, and my Marines lifted the siege of the consulate. The Flag Captain Percival Jenkins walked over for orders. Kincaid said: "Signal USS Petrel and *USS Concord* to escort *Nanshan* and *Sapiro* into the Bay, through the south channel and dock where Commodore Dewey directs." Kincaid then thanked Von Diederichs for his concerns and escorted him to the motorized barge back to his flagship. The German East Asiatic Fleet then departed.

Admiral Kincaid ordered the balance of the fleet into Manila Bay. The first order of business was clearing the mines out of the north channel. The next day, USS Concord and USS McCulloch carrying duplicate dispatches steamed out of Manila Bay to Pearl Harbor.

Three weeks later, an alliance between the United States Marines and the remaining Spanish Garrison drove the rebels 50-miles away from Manila. Leaving Commodore Dewey's cruiser squadron, and three-thousand Marines as a garrison, Admiral Kincaid left Manila Bay and steamed to Pearl Harbor.

The new United States Secretary of State, John Hay entered into negotiations to purchase the Philippine archipelago and the Island of Guam from Spain. The Spanish government was in turmoil as King Alfonso XII died and his wife; Queen Maria Christina was pregnant with a hoped male heir. Months later she gave birth to Alfonso XIII and was declared Queen-Regent until the infant king reached majority.

John Hay was very persuasive noting that Spain was unable to defend her Pacific Oceania possessions. Hay, who previously was the Ambassador to the United Kingdom, had a very amicable relationship with the British foreign service. The British, concerned that if the United States left the Philippines, the German Empire would take over, supported Hay's efforts.

The treaty signing took place on April 15, 1899. The United States paid Spain the sum of twenty million dollars and paid for the removal of the Spanish garrisons and their dependents. On June 2, 1899, in a ceremony in Manilla, the last Spanish Governor-General Diego de los Rios lowered the Spanish Flag in Manila and watched as the Stars and Stripes rose up the flagstaff. With bands playing, the Spanish garrison marched onto troopships and steamed for home.

The Philippine rebel leaders wrote a Constitution and declared the Philippine Republic on January 21, 1899. The United

States and all the other nations refused recognition. On June 2, 1899, in response to the United States purchase, and refusal to recognize Philippine independence, the Philippine Republic declared war on the United States.

The Philippine-American War lasted until July 2, 1902, first with pitched battles, then guerrilla warfare. Major fighting ended with the capture of the Philippine President Emilio Aguinaldo on March 23, 1901, and the collapse of the Philippine government in 1902.

The arrest, trial, imprisonment and subsequent execution of Aguinaldo's self-proclaimed successor Macario Sakay on September 13, 1907, reduced the war to irregular guerrilla warfare. The Battle of Bud Basak on June 13, 1913, ended with the annihilation of the last of the Moro rebels by a combined American and Filipino army led by Black Jack Pershing.

The war cost the United States army over

15,000 casualties, including over 5,000 dead. The brutal guerilla warfare resulted in atrocities from both sides, including the massacre of whole villages, and the torture and execution of prisoners.

The war changed the cultural landscape of the islands. The conflict resulted in the deaths of an estimated 25,000 Filipino soldiers, and 200,000 to 250,000 Filipino civilians. The introduction of freedom of religion ended the role of the Catholic Church as the state religion. English became the primary language of government, education, business, industry, and among families of educated individuals. English became the primary language taught in public schools.

A census took place in 1903. Elections for the Philippine Assembly took place in 1904. That assembly consisted of eighty elected representatives, empowered to handle local legislative matters. The Assembly changed the name of their body to the House of Representatives. The American Governor appointed an upper chamber which served as the Senate. The House voted on and approved a Bill of Rights for Filipino citizens, and the Governor signed it into law. The House and Senate also elected two non-voting representatives to attend the United States Congress.

Democrats in the United States heavily criticized American Imperialism. They often quoted George Washington's caution against foreign entanglements. Democrat newspapers lampooned with editorials and cartoons.

COLOSSUS OF THE PACIFIC

Republicans ridiculed the Democrats as isolationists, who were out of step with the realities of the modern age.

Chapter 13

China Crisis

China had become a significant trading partner for Western nations, and for Japan. China lacked the military muscle to resist incursions by these countries, and several, including Russia at Port Arthur, Britain at Hong Kong, and Germany at Tientsin, carved off bits of China as Treaty Ports.

The controlling nations used the ports as trading centers and military bases. Within those jurisdictions, the country in possession gave preference to its citizens in trade and the development of infrastructures such as railroads, churches, schools, and hospitals. The Chinese were on the outside looking in, within their own nation.

Although the United States did not claim any parts of China, United States-flagged ships carried a third of the China trade. Having an outpost in the Far East became a significant factor in the decision to obtain a base of operations in the Philippines.

As Secretary of State, it was Hay's responsibility to put together a workable China policy. Charles Beresford, a British Member of Parliament, met with Hay, who introduced him to President McKinley. In that meeting, an Open Door Policy developed.

The Open Door policy assured that all nations would agree to an even playing field in China. That would give the foreign powers little incentive to dismember the Chinese Empire through territorial acquisition.

Concerned that the Senate would object, Hay convinced McKinley to formally issue his Open Door Executive Order on September 6, 1899. The policy was not a treaty and did not require the approval of the Senate. Most of the powers had at least some caveats, and negotiations continued through the remainder of the year. On March 20, 1900, Hay announced that all the delegations had agreed, and he was not contradicted.

The Boxer Rebellion.

The Chinese reaction to the Open Door Policy quickly became violent. Strong opposition opposed Western influence. A movement in Shantung province became known as the Fists of Righteous Harmony, or Boxers, after the martial arts they practiced.

The presence of missionaries and their converts, especially angered the Boxers. By the middle of June, the Boxers, joined by imperial troops, had cut the railroad between Peking and the coast. They killed hundreds of missionaries and converts and besieged the compound housing the foreign legations.

McKinley faced a precarious situation; how to rescue the Americans trapped in Peking, and how to avoid giving the other powers an excuse to partition China. It was an election year where already the Democrat opposition and their newspapers criticized what they deemed American imperialism.

McKinley sent American troops from the Philippines to China to relieve the nation's legation. He instructed Hay to make all possible efforts preserve to the Open Door Policy. On July 3, 1900, Hay sent a letter to foreign powers stating while the United States wanted to see lives protected and the guilty punished, the United States intended to prevent the dismemberment of China.

Communication between the foreign legations and the outside world had been cut off, and the personnel there were presumed slaughtered. Hay realized that the Chinese Ambassador Wu Ting-fang could communicate with his Foreign Office, and used Wu to talk directly to the Chinese government. Ambassador Wu informed him the legations were under siege, but still intact.

Hay 's diplomacy convinced the Chinese government that it now needed to cooperate as a condition of its survival. The Dowager Empress instructed the Imperial Troops to stand down. The Boxers abandoned by the Imperial Army faced annihilation when the international relief force, principally Japanese but including 2,000 Americans, relieved the legations. The victors sacked Peking, and China was made to pay a huge indemnity. However, there was no partition of the country

Chapter 14

Election of 1900

On June 19 to 21 the Republican Convention re-nominated William McKinley by acclamation. They also nominated first-term Governor of New York as Vice President on the first ballot. Roosevelt was a reformer, and party leaders wanted him out of the way. Roosevelt initially resisted the nomination as he considered the Vice Presidency to be a powerless office. Ultimately he accepted.

The Republicans campaigned on a booming economy, a strong dollar and respect from abroad. Roosevelt barnstormed across twenty-three states, making four-hundred and eighty whistle stops. McKinley again campaigned from his front porch, receiving delegations of thousands of voters.

The Democrats again nominated William Jennings Bryan, who also received the nomination of the Populists and Anti-Imperialism Parties. Their Vice Presidential nominee was Adlai Stevenson, who was Grover Cleveland's Vice President during his second term.

The Democrats campaigned on free silver, the end of the gold standard. They also heavily criticized the Republican imperialistic war in the Philippines. He accused McKinley of replacing a brutal Spanish regime with a cruel American one.

The final vote total gave McKinley a plurality more than one and one-half million popular votes. McKinley also won 332 Electoral votes. He won 34 states including the northeast and midwest, the west coast, the Caribbean, Ontario, Quebec, Nova Scotia, and New Brunswick.

The Democrats under William Jennings Bryan won only 155 Electoral votes. Bryan took the Democrat stronghold in the south and a few farm states.

In the Congressional elections, the Republicans won 221 seats, the Democrats 155, the Populists five, and the Parti Patriote nine. The Republicans, by being victorious in thirty-four states increased their total to a 20 seat majority in the Senate following senatorial selection of expiring terms in the 1901 state legislatures.

Democrat influence slowly diminished with the depopulation of the southern states. Over the past twenty-five years, more than ninety-five percent of the black population had relocated to the Caribbean or joined relatives in Liberia. That decreased the overall population in that region by one-third, and those states were losing representatives with each census.

Migration to the West complicated the issue. Poor whites, seeing little incentive to stay in the south migrated west. There they could homestead on 160 acres of land. Wealthy landowners were finding fewer and fewer people to work their land. Many began to import migrant workers and their families from Mexico.

The Inauguration of William McKinley took place on March 4, 1901. Patriotic fervor surrounded the ceremonies. The new Vice President Theodore Roosevelt was very popular. The economy was growing, and prosperity was spreading. However, political discord was still apparent, with sharp divides between the Democrat-dominated south, and the Republican domination of most the rest of the country.

At the Inaugural Ball following the inauguration, McKinley and Roosevelt stood before a large mural of the United States of America. The map showed the United States dominating all of North America, plus the Caribbean states of Domenica, Puerto Rico, and Cuba. Only Mexico remained independent.

In thirty-five years, the United States had grown from a country torn by civil war to the dominant nation in the Western Hemisphere. Internationally, the United States was universally respected, and by some nations feared. With overseas possessions in Hawaii, the Philippines, and Guam, the United States was also an imperial power. A fleet of modern battleships projected this power.

In Africa, a firm alliance with Liberia cemented relations. Trade was brisk between the two nations. Liberia's Navy still employed a cadre of former United States Navy officers, paying a premium salary to entice recruitment. However, many of these senior officers were teaching in the Liberian Naval War College. Most of the junior officers, graduates of the College, were Liberian born. The United States still constructed Liberian warships, mostly fast or armored cruisers to protect their burgeoning maritime enterprises.

Chapter 15

Panama Canal:

The French efforts to construct a ground-level canal in Columbia's province of Panama were a total failure. Excavation began in 1881, but immediately encountered problems with Yellow Fever, avalanches, and collapse from mudslides and dynamite explosions. Of the 50,000 employees, 22,000 died from disease or accidents. Over 5,000 of those were French engineers. With the death toll escalating, qualified engineers refused to apply. The Panama Company went bankrupt in 1889. The French Parliament undertook a 4-year investigation which revealed the problems stemmed from massive corruption involving 104 legislatures.

With new funding appropriated, construction resumed in 1894. However little progress occurred due to aging equipment and lack of workers. The Panama Canal Company entered its second bankruptcy.

With little progress in sixteen years, Columbia voided the contract. The United States Secretary of State John Hay entered into negotiations to assume the lease. The new plans were for two pairs locks to raise and lower vessels during the transit, and the creation of an artificial lake by damming the Chagres River.

For the United States to legally build a canal in Central America, Hay had to abrogate the *Clayton-Bulwer Treaty* between the United States and the United Kingdom, which explicitly forbade either nation to construct a channel they exclusively controlled.

Public opinion in the United States had been growing over the Clayton–Bulwer Treaty's restriction on that country's independent action. The British recognized their diminishing influence in the region and determined to cultivate the United States to counterbalance Germany's diplomatic efforts in Central and South America.

Secretary Hay and the British Ambassador Lord Pauncefote open new negotiations in December 1990. Pauncefote's instructions from the Foreign Office indicated he could concede anything but the neutrality of access. Negotiations were lengthy, and the final version of the treaty was provided to McKinley to sign on November 8, 1901. McKinley sent it to the Senate which ratified it on December 16, 1901.

The Hay–Pauncefote Treaty abrogated the *Clayton–Bulwer Treaty*. It did not prohibit the United States from constructing fortifications and did not require the United States to keep the canal open in time of war. The Treaty ceded to the United States the right to build and manage the channel provided that all nations would be allowed access.

The next step was to negotiate a treaty with Columbia, which ruled Panama as a province. In January 1903, John Hay entered into negotiations with the Columbian Ambassador Thomas Herran. The *Hay-Herran Treaty* provided for a $10,000,000 payment in gold coin plus an annual rent of $250,000. The United States Senate ratified the treaty on March 14. However, on August 12, the agreement was rejected by the Congress of Colombia, even though the Colombian government proposed the terms.

Unwilling to renegotiate, the United States covertly supported the Panamanian rebellion, which began on July 24, 1903, when the Colombian Army assaulted El Lapiz newspaper building. The separatists in Panama rose up and defeated the Colombian garrison troops.

The United States sent naval forces to delay the Columbian Army from sending reinforcements. Upon arrival, that army mostly Panamanians, led by General Esteban Huertas mutinied and joined the rebellion. On November 4, the Panamanians declared their independence and formed a provisional government, which was immediately recognized by the United States.

On November 18, 1903, the ratification of *Hay-Buena Varilla Treaty* took place. That treaty guaranteed the independence of Panama and provided the United States total sovereignty over a ten-mile wide canal zone in perpetuity. The terms of payment were identical to the terms of the *Hay-Harran Treaty*.

Carnegie Hall

John Phillip Sousa scheduled a New Years Eve concert and invited the President and his wife to attend. Secretary of State John Hay, on his way to New Hampshire, accompanied the Presidential Party. President McKinley and his wife Ida sat in the Presidential box and enthusiastically applauded the patriotic music. Before conducting the Grand Finale with his famous march *STARS AND STRIPES FOREVER,* Sousa paused and saluted

President McKinley and his wife. With the capacity crowd on their feet and loudly applauding Sousa's band played the march. Three encores of Sousa's other famous marches followed, with the final playing of *STARS AND STRIPES FOREVER.* President McKinley and Ida were on their feet cheering as loudly as the audience.

Mckinley and Ida were talking animatedly about the music as they left Carnegie Hall and approached their carriage. Mckinley was heard to say: "That was the best musical performance of my life." Suddenly three shots were fired. Two struck Mckinley in the chest; one hit Ida in the neck. Bleeding heavily, both collapsed on the stairs. McKinley reached over and grasped Ida's hand, their eyes locked, McKinley mouthed: "I love you," then Ida died.

The assassin Leon Czolgosz, an anarchist was pounced upon by the crowd and beaten senseless before being hauled away to the local precinct by New York Police. There he was viciously beaten with batons before being tossed into a cell.

Police rushed McKinley to New York General Hospital where he underwent emergency surgery. He never regained consciousness and died at 7 am.

At 9 am on January 1, 1904, John Hay's carriage pulled up to Vice President Roosevelt's home, Sagamore Hills, in Oyster Bay New York. Accompanying Hay was the Honorable John A Hazel, a District Court Judge. The Vice President, his wife Edith and six children were having breakfast. Looking at John Hay's downcast demeanor, Theodore asked: Mr. Secretary, what has happened." Hay Replied.

"Mr. President, President McKinley and Ida were shot last night as they left Carnegie Hall. Ida died at the scene. The President died at 7 am this morning. Judge Hazel is here to administer to you the oath of office." With his family looking on, President Theodore Roosevelt placed his left hand on his family Bible, raised his right hand and repeated: “I Theodore Roosevelt do solemnly swear…..”

Nine days after the funerals, Czolgosz went on trial for two counts of first-degree murder. He stood mute during his hearing and did not cooperate with his defense attorneys. The jury convicted him, and the judge sentenced him to death by electrocution. Five weeks later Czolgosz was executed in the electric chair.

The Republican establishment expressed dismay about Roosevelt becoming the President. In 1899, New York’s Lemuel Quigg and Thomas Platt initially convinced Roosevelt to enter politics and run for Governor. He won narrowly but then disappointed the party bosses by taxing corporations and opposing trusts.

Roosevelt gained wide popularity with twice-daily news conferences, which connected him with middle-class voters. At the Republican Convention, Platt and Quigg convinced him to accept the Vice

Presidency. They hoped that nominating him Vice President at the convention in 1900 would sideline him.

On the other hand, McKinley's campaign manager Senator Mark Hanna from Ohio vigorously opposed Roosevelt's nomination. When Roosevelt's nomination became inevitable, Hanna replied to the question: W*hat was the matter*? Hanna responded:

"*Matter! Matter! Why everybody's gone crazy! What is the matter with all of you? Here this convention is going headlong for Roosevelt for Vice President. Don't any of you realize that there's only one life between that madman and the Presidency? Platt and Quigg are no better than idiots! What harm can he do as Governor of New York compared to the damage he will do as President if McKinley should die*"?

McKinley's death left Hanna devastated both personally and politically. As the leader of the conservative wing of the party, and a close associate of McKinley, he was the most likely Republican Party candidate for President as McKinley previously indicated he would not run for a third term.

Roosevelt reached out to Hanna, hoping to secure his influence in the Senate. Hanna indicated that he was willing to come to terms with Roosevelt on two conditions. First, that Roosevelt would continue McKinley's political agenda; and second that the President cease from his habit of calling Hanna *old man*, something which much annoyed the senator. Hanna warned Roosevelt, "If you don't, I'll call you Teddy." Roosevelt, who despised his nickname, agreed to both terms.

Their alliance would not last long. On January 30, 1904, Mark Hanna contracted Typhoid Fever. As his condition worsened, Roosevelt visited him on February 15. Hanna was semi-conscious. Roosevelt tried to encourage, indicating he was looking forward to Hanna's advice and support in the coming Presidential campaign. Hanna died at 6 pm that evening. With the death of Hanna, there were no other potential candidates to oppose Roosevelt.

Chapter 16

The election of 1904

The Republican Convention convened in Chicago on June 21 – 23. Roosevelt's nomination was assured. He won the nomination on the first ballot, collecting all 994 votes. Roosevelt realized that to unite the party; he needed a conservative as the Vice Presidential nominee. Many conservatives viewed Roosevelt as a radical. He wisely let them choose among themselves their favorite nominee. The conservatives nominated Charles W Fairbanks on the first ballot.

The platform became the next order of business. The platform planks insisted on the following.

1. The continuation of protective tariffs.
2. Called for an increase in foreign trade.
3. Vowed to uphold the gold standard.

4. Favored the expansion of the merchant marine.
5. Promoted a strong navy.
6. Praised in detail Roosevelt's continuation of McKinley's foreign and domestic policies.

The Democrat Party convention convened in St. Louis from July 6 – 9. In the months leading up to their conclave, the Democrats fractionalized, resulting in a deep split between the conservative Bourbon Democrats and the progressive/populist wing. William Jennings Bryan, the twice defeated candidate in 1896 and 1900, declined to run for the nomination. He however worked against the party's interest by trying to get the weakest candidate nominated. That way he could retain control of the party.

The progressives turned to Representative William Randolph Hearst, the owner of eight newspapers. Hearst, whose papers vigorously supported W.J Bryan in 1896 and

1900 hoped for Bryans endorsement. Instead, Bryan endorsed Hearst's populist rival Francis Cockrell, the four-time Senator from Missouri.

The other leading candidate was Judge Alton Parker of New York. Parker's main attributes were that being out of politics for twenty years, he did not have political enemies. Bryan despised him as Parker had ruled the law mandating the 8-hour workday law in New York unconstitutional.

Conservatives, so alarmed that Hearst could get the nomination coalesced around Parker. On the first ballot, Parker received 658 votes, nine votes less than the required two-thirds majority. Before the announcement of the ballot count, the party bosses met behind closed doors. Following the meeting, 21 additional votes switched in Parker's favor.

Bryan continued to work behind the scenes to hinder Parker. Knowing that Parker favored the Gold Standard; Bryan inserted a plank that the platform support bimetallism. Upon hearing of Bryan's meddling, Parker threatened to decline the nomination. Fearing a debacle if Parker withdrew, after the rancorous debate, the convention voted to remove bimetallism from the platform. Bryan was outraged and charged that the trusts engineered the change, and secured it by crooked and indefensible means.

The Democrats nominated West Virginia's Senator Henry Davis as Vice President. They hoped he could deliver his state. Davis also owned mines, railroads and was a banker.

The Democrat platform included the following planks.

1. Reduction in government spending
2. Breakup of monopolies
3. Opposition to imperialism
4. Independence of the Philippines
5. Opposition to Tariffs
6. Enforcement of 8-hour workday

Two other parties participated in the elections. The Socialists nominated Eugene Debbs, and the Prohibitionist nominated Silas Swallow.

On election day, the Roosevelt – Fairbanks ticket won 58 percent of the popular votes, and 366 electoral votes, including all the states except for the "Solid South." Missouri broke ranks in the south and voted for Roosevelt. The Parker – Davis ticket won 37 percent of the vote and 140 electoral votes. The socialists won 3 percent of the vote, and the Prohibitionists won 2 percent. With such a massive landslide, Roosevelt eagerly looked forward to using his mandate.

In the congressional elections, the Republicans picked up 41 seats and increased their total to 272. The Democrat lost 46 seats reducing their total to 135. With seventy-five percent of their seats located in the deep south; the Democrat Party looked more and more like a regional party.

The Populists lost all their seats, and the Parti Patriote increased their representation to 10 seats by capturing the last previously Democrat seats in New Brunswick, Nova Scotia, and Ontario.

The Caribbean states were solidly Republican and developed a distinctly Caribbean culture. The population was a mix of Hispanic, white industrial workers from the north and a massive influx of blacks from the south. The construction of water, sewer and sanitation systems; and the extensive use of DDT largely eradicated diseases such as Yellow Fever, Malaria, and Typhoid.

Mandatory childhood attendance in public schools, with English as the primary language, created a literate and educated population. Religious freedom fostered rapid church growth and high levels of participation. The Catholic churches predominated. However, multiple Protestant denominations experienced rapid growth. With booming economies in the three states, the various cultures blended in a unique mosaic.

Chapter 17

Roosevelt's first foray into foreign relations came from the Russo-Japanese war of 1904 - 05. For over five years, tensions between the two nations rose over the Russian occupation of Manchuria, and their naval base at Port Arthur. That directly threatened Japanese control of Korea.

Months of negotiations ensued with little progress. Tsar Nicholas II was encouraged to stand fast by his cousin Kaiser William II, who referred to the Japanese and Chinese as the *Yellow Peril*. Japan and Great Britain were allies, with the British building many of the Japanese warships. That alliance also included a mutual defense treaty.

With negotiations at a standstill, Japan broke off diplomatic relations with Russia. On February 4, 1904, Japan declared war on Russia. Three hours before the declaration reached the Russian diplomats, the Imperial Japanese Navy attacked Port

Arthur with a flotilla of destroyers firing torpedos. The attack damaged two Russian Navy battleships and a cruiser. Additional naval battles fought around Port Arthur over the next two days proved to be indecisive.

The Russian Far East Army invaded Korea and advanced past Seoul. The Japanese Imperial Army (JIA) defeated the poorly equipped Russian army and gradually drove it back. In a protracted and costly campaign, the JIA drove the Russians out of Korea, then besieged Port Arthur.

The Russians responded by sending their Baltic fleet of eleven battleships and eight cruisers to relieve Port Arthur. The British closed the Suez Canal to the Russians after the Russian Navy fired on British fishing boats at Dogger Bank, mistaking them for Japanese torpedo boats. The Russians then sailed around Africa, a journey taking several months. By the time the Russian Fleet arrived, Port Arthur had fallen.

The climactic battle of the war occurred at

Tsushima Strait on May 27 & 28 1905. There the Imperial Japanese Navy destroyed the Russian fleet, sinking four cruisers, seven battleships, capturing four. Four other Russian warships escaped.

Japan extended initial peace efforts for a negotiated settlement, by the United States, on March 8, 1905. On paper, they were winning the war. However, economic conditions and mounting debt discouraged a long, drawn-out conflict. When contacted through diplomatic channels, Tsar Nicholas II refused to negotiate believing Russia would win a long drawn out fight.

The Battle of Tsushima Strait changed his mind. On June 8, Tsar Nicholas agreed to peace negotiations. Roosevelt scheduled the peace conference in Portsmouth, NH.

Foreign Minister Kromura Jutaro, assisted by the ambassador to Washington Takahira Kogoro led the Japanese delegation. The Finance Minister Sergei Witte, supported by former ambassador to Japan Roman

Rosen, and international law and arbitration specialist Friedrich Martens led the Russian delegation. There were twelve sessions held between August 9 and August 30.

During the first eight sessions, the delegates were able to reach an agreement on several points. These included:

An immediate cease-fire.

Russia's recognition of Japan's claims to Korea.

The evacuation of Russian forces from Manchuria.

Russia was also required to return its leases in southern Manchuria containing Port Arthur and Talien to China.

Russia required to turn over the South Manchuria Railway and its mining concessions to Japan.

Russia was allowed to retain the Chinese Eastern Railway in northern Manchuria.

The remaining four sessions addressed the most challenging issues, those of reparations and territorial concessions. On August 18, Roosevelt proposed that Rosen offer to divide the island of Sakhalin to address the territory issue. The Japanese previously captured the island as a bargaining chip.

On August 23, however, Witte proposed that the Japanese keep Sakhalin and drop their claims for reparations. When Komura rejected this proposal, Witte warned that he was instructed to cease negotiations and that the war would resume.

This ultimatum came as four new Russian divisions arrived in Manchuria, and the Russian delegation made an ostentatious show of packing their bags and preparing to depart. Witte was convinced that the Japanese could not afford to restart the war. He applied pressure via the American media and his American hosts to persuade the Japanese that the monetary compensation issue was something that

Russia would never compromise.

Outmaneuvered by Witte, Komura yielded, and in exchange for the southern half of Sakhalin, the Japanese dropped their claims for reparations.

The signing of the Treaty of Portsmouth occurred on September 5, 1905. The Japanese Privy Council ratified the treaty on October 10, and the Tsar in Russia on October 14, 1905.

Because of the role played by President Theodore Roosevelt, the United States became a significant force in world diplomacy. Roosevelt was awarded the Nobel Peace Prize in 1906 for his back-channel efforts before and during the peace negotiations, even though he never actually went to Portsmouth.

The United States Navy War College studied the Battle of Tsushima Straights. The (*IJN*) Imperial Japanese Navy's victory elevated them on the potential threat board.

After considerable study and wargaming, the college determined several factors which contributed to the Japanese success. Their report to the Department of the Navy contained assessments and recommendations.

First, the *IJN* numerous naval battles with Russia's Far East Fleet honed their command structure and gunnery skills.

Second, the *IJN* utilized modern range-finding equipment with effective targeting up to 6,000 meters. The Russian Navy used an older model of rangefinders with effective targeting up to 4,000 meters.

Third, the *IJN* had a unified command, whereas the Russian command structure was divided.

Fourth, the *IJN* utilized high explosive rounds which exploded on impact. The Russian Navy employed armor-piercing shells, which often failed to explode due to defective fuses.

Fifth, the Russian Admirals failed to appropriately respond to Admiral Togo's crossing their T. They ordered a general melee instead of a line abreast formation which would have enabled all of the Russian forward guns to be brought into action at the same time. The line abreast formation is also easily converted to a parallel battle line. The general melee order allowed the *IJN* battle line to target Russian battleships individually.

The War College recommendations included new battleship construction with the positioning of two, triple gun turrets forward in a super firing position, with the number two turret elevated and positioned behind the first. This arrangement would increase the firepower of the line abreast formation.

The second recommendation suggested an increase in the gun dimensions from the current 12-inch to 14-inch or even 16-inch. The new caliber of guns would increase the range of active combat and the destructive power of impact.

The Department of the Navy accepted the recommendations and agreed to incorporate them into future battleship designs.

Chapter 18

The Royal Navy began construction of HMS Dreadnought on October 2, 1905. Launched on February 10, 1906, and commissioned on December 2, 1906, HMS Dreadnought became the first all big gun battleship. Her armament included five, twin 12-inch gun turrets.

The launching and commissioning of HMS Dreadnought caused all the other battleships to be obsolete. The term "Dreadnought" became widely used to differentiate the older battleships, now called pre-Dreadnoughts, from the newer battleship designs. The European powers, notably the German Empire, engaged in a building frenzy, each competing to gain parity or supremacy over the Royal Navy.

The United States Navy expedited construction on the two South Carolina Class battleships. Production delays and testing of the superfiring turrets had slowed completion. However, with new urgency, the commissioning ceremony for USS South Carolina occurred on March 31, 1907. Sea trials began immediately. Her sister ship, the USS Michigan joined the fleet on July 1.

There were significant differences between the HMS Dreadnought and the South Carolina Class battleships. HMS Dreadnought's five turrets were arranged one forward, one in the stern, one midship, and two on the wings, one starboard, and the other port. The barbettes that housed the turrets were flush with the deck. That meant that the stern and the midship guns could not be fired in the same direction simultaneously. Her main advantage was speed. HMS Dreadnought could cruise at 21 knots.

The South Carolina Class battleships advantage concerned the arrangement of the turrets. With superfiring guns fore and aft, all their guns could fire in the same direction simultaneously. Their main disadvantage was speed. With a maximum speed of 18 knots, they could be outdistanced and outmaneuvered by HMS Dreadnought, and subsequent Royal Navy Dreadnoughts.

HMS Dreadnought

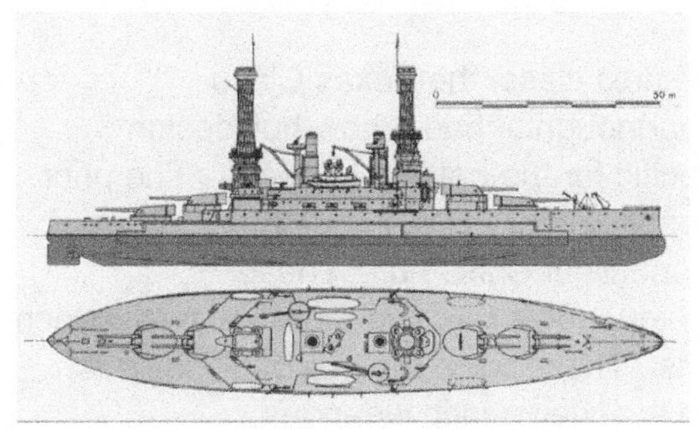

USS South Carolina

During the next ten years, the United States Navy built twenty-two Dreadnoughts, with incremental improvements with each class. The next Dreadnoughts, the Delaware Class, substituted turbine engines for the triple-expansion steam engines and added three knots of speed.

The Florida Class were sixty feet longer than the Delaware Class, which allowed for the addition of a fifth midships turret. The next battleships, the Wyoming class, lengthened the vessels another fifty feet and added a second midships turret in a superfiring position.

The next class, the Texas Class Dreadnoughts, had a new hull design specific for the battleship needs. The prior Dreadnoughts used an enlarged Connecticut Class hull. These Dreadnoughts had five turrets of twelve-inch guns. These were the last battleships to use the twelve-inch weapons.

The next six Dreadnoughts were of standard design, utilizing the concept of customization to speed construction and to use the Panama Canal locks, which were 110 feet in width. The battleships were 624 feet long and 103 feet at the beam. The added length allowed them to carry four, triple gun turrets with the new fourteen-inch guns, which were the most massive turrets and cannons of any existing United States Navy battleships.

Chapter 19

Election of 1908

The election marked the entry of two new states, Oklahoma and Columbia, into the presidential campaign; both joined the union in 1907.

Oklahoma was originally the home to the Osage and the Quapaw native tribes. It was commonly called Indian Territory. President Andrew Jackson forcefully settled five native tribes, plus their black slaves from east of the Mississippi to Indian Territory in the 1830s during the *Trail of Tears*. The tribes joined the Confederacy. After the end of the Civil War, the tribes were forced to free their slaves in 1866.

Attempts to create an all-Indian state named *Sequoyah* failed, but the Sequoyah Statehood Convention of 1905 eventually laid the groundwork for the Oklahoma Statehood Convention, which took place two years later. On November 16, 1907, Oklahoma became the fifty-third state in the Union.

Migrants from Oregon, Washington, and California moved to Columbia shortly after the expulsion of the British. The Hudson Bay Company tried to exert control, as previously before British Columbia became a province, it was under Hudson Bay administration.

The lower courts ruled against the Company. Several appeals later, the Supreme Court, based its decision on the wording of the Annexation Treaty. *The Hudson Bay Company will sign a deal of surrender. The Company will retain ownership of Rupert's Land and administration of their territory but must surrender sovereignty to the United States of America.*

As Columbia was not part of Rupert's Land at the time of the treaty, the Supreme Court, in a unanimous decision, affirmed the lower court rulings that the Company did not have an ownership or administrative rights. The court also established the northern border of the territory at the 54th parallel on the north, the Washington border on the south, and the continental divide on the east.

With the final court ruling, President Grant appointed General George Crook as territorial Governor. Crook moved the regional capital from Victoria to Vancouver. Grant extended the Homestead Act to the territory, and settlers began to migrate in and establish farms.

The Northern Pacific Railroad laid track to Vancouver, which expedited settlement. In 1905 a plebiscite, to officially name the territory, selected Columbia over North Washington. That plebiscite paved the way for the Columbia Statehood Convention. On December 1, 1907, Columbia became the fifty-fourth state in the Union.

The Republicans held their convention from June 16 to 19 in Chicago. The ticket of

Roosevelt and Fairbanks were re-nominated by acclamation. The platform touted Roosevelt's accomplishments at home and in foreign policy, notably his Nobel Peace Prize for facilitating the Treaty of Portsmouth. Domestically a strong economy fueled business expansion. Charles Fairbanks anchored the conservative wing of the party.

The Democrats held their convention in Denver between July 7 and 10. William Jennings Bryan won by acclamation and selected John Kern from Indiana as his running mate. Without the Free Silver issue, Bryan campaigned on a progressive platform attacking "government by privilege." His campaign slogan, "Shall the People Rule" was featured on numerous posters and campaign memorabilia. However, Roosevelt's progressive policies undercut Bryan's liberal support and blurred the distinctions between the parties. Republicans also used the slogan "Vote for Roosevelt now, you can vote for Bryan anytime." That remark brought out loud cheers at Roosevelt rallies as it was a sharp reminder of Bryan's two previously failed presidential campaigns.

On November 3, the final tally gave the Roosevelt – Fairbanks ticket 54 percent of the vote. The Bryan – Kern ticket won 40 percent. Oklahoma voted for Bryan, Columbia voted for Roosevelt. The Socialists won 3 percent, and other minor parties won a total of two percent. The Electoral College vote gave Roosevelt 371 votes and Bryan 172 votes. After his third defeat, Bryan vowed never again run for elected office. He remained the leader of the progressive wing of the Democrat party.

In the Congressional elections, the Republicans won 263 seats, and the Democrats won 172. The Parti-Patriote retained their ten seats.

Chapter 20

Roosevelt's second full term began with an economy recovering from the Panic of 1907. The panic occurred during three weeks in October. The stock market lost almost fifty percent compared with the previous year peak. It started with the failure of the Knickerbocker Trust company, the third-largest bank in New York. Knickerbocker attempted to corner the market on stock of the United Copper Company. To do so, it borrowed large sums of money from other major banks. The takeover failed, and Knickerbocker became insolvent.

The bank runs started on Knickerbocker and its affiliated banks. Soon the runs hit the banks which loaned Knickerbocker money as depositors feared the banks did not have enough money to cover their deposits. Historians credit J.P. Morgan with ending the panic by infusing millions of dollars into the banks while encouraging other wealthy financiers to do the same. With liquidity restored, the bank runs ended.

Roosevelt formed a commission to provide recommendations on how to stop the bank runs and panics which periodically plagued the economy. After two years of study, the commission recommended a quasi-governmental agency to regulate the banks. Roosevelt's congressional allies proposed legislation to establish such an agency. Following much debate, Congress created the Federal Reserve System.

Roosevelt became an activist in domestic and foreign affairs. His activities became known as The Big Stick Policy. The policy named after one of his favorite quotes stated: "Speak softly and carry a big stick. You will go far." The idea was to speak softly in a non-aggressive manner, but always hold open the option for aggressive behavior. He used this in domestic affairs with his policies of busting trusts and opposing union strikes.

Roosevelt applied Big Stick Diplomacy in foreign relations with his promotion of the rapid increases in the number, size, and quality of the United States Navy

Dreadnought battleships. He based the Navy's African Squadron in Monrovia, as a clear reminder that Liberia remained as a protectorate of the United States.

Roosevelt faced a crisis in Mexico in 1909. He sponsored a summit meeting with Mexican President Porfirio Diaz in El Passo Texas. The summit aimed to shore up support for President Diaz and to protect the over nine billion dollars in American investments in Mexico. Diaz faced increased opposition to his twenty-five-year Presidency.

On October 16, both presidents narrowly escaped assassination when a Texas Ranger saw a man standing on the parade route palming a pistol. The Ranger confronted and arrested the would-be assassin moments before the open vehicle containing Roosevelt and Diaz drove past.

Diaz experienced a convoluted path to the presidency of Mexico. In February 1870 Maximillian, leading his victorious army marched into Mexico City. President Benito Juarez was dead. His army betrayed and executed him in the public square.

General Diaz, head of the last army opposing Maximillian sent a message seeking terms of surrender. Maximillian provided safe-conduct for Diaz to travel to Mexico City. There he knelt before his Emperor, kissed his ring, and pledged his loyalty. Maximillian accepted Diaz's pledge of allegiance and allowed him to retire to his estates in Oaxaca.

Maximillian died of cancer in 1876. His heir and adopted son Salvador de Iturbide succeeded him as Emperor. Salvador, unlike Maximillian, had little interest in governing. He invited Diaz to return from retirement and resume political life. In 1878, Diaz's Nationalist Party won the congressional elections. The Emperor appointed him Prime Minister. Mexico, being a constitutional monarchy, allowed the prime minister and the Congress to run the day to day functioning of the government. Salvador became content to attend ceremonial functions, and entertain visiting heads of state.

The former Empress Carlotta sank into a deep depression following the death of Maximillian. Late in 1881, with hopes of curing her distress, the Royal Family including Salvador, his wife Empress Giselle, his daughter Maria, and Carlotta sailed for an extended visit to Europe. Following more than a year of the absence of the Royal Family, Diaz planned a peaceful coup.

Initially, Diaz planted stories and editorials in the newspapers lamenting the absence of the Emperor. Within several months discontent with the monarchy grew, and anti-monarchy demonstrations broke out. Diaz then publically broke with the monarchy and accused Salvador of abandoning his responsibilities to the people of Mexico.

Congress then overwhelmingly passed legislation dissolving the monarchy; declared Mexico a republic, and scheduled elections. Diaz, as Prime Minister, and the leader of the largest political party governed until he was elected President of Mexico.

The exiled former Emperor Salvador, without substantial political or military support, signed a treaty with Diaz. In return for one million dollars in gold, he formally abdicated the crown. The Mexican Congress, glad not to have to face another civil war, ratified the treaty.

During his first term in office, Diaz developed a pragmatic approach to solve political conflicts. Although a political liberal who supported radical extremist elements in Oaxaca, he eschewed the liberal ideologues. Diaz maintained control through generous patronage to political allies. Even though Diaz ruled as an authoritarian, he continued the structure of elections. That established the façade of liberal democracy.

Diaz secured United States government recognition of his regime, even though it came to power by a coup. Mexican Congressional approval and the later niceties of an election helped. Mexico also paid $300,000 to settle bandit raid claims by the United States. In 1884, the United States recognized the legitimacy of the Diaz government. As a show of goodwill, former United States President Ulysses S. Grant visited Mexico.

Once secure in his power, Diaz took control of the electoral process. Friends and associates ran for offices and were elected as governors and mayors throughout Mexico. The Federal Army generals were his devoted followers. The Army quickly suppressed any revolts. For the next twenty-six years, presidential election results announced his almost unanimous re-election.

In 1910, Diaz allowed Francisco Madero, an aristocrat with democratic leanings to run against him. Despite gathering a considerable following, the announced results reelected Diaz, with only a few votes for Madero. Decrying the election fraud, Madero called for a revolt, which spread throughout Mexico. The Federal Army, weakened by corruption proved itself unable to contain the insurgency. Following repeated defeats to the Army, Diaz signed the *Treaty of Ciudad Juarez.* He and his vice-president abdicated power and accepted exile in Spain.

The abdication of the Diaz government presented a serious foreign policy issue for Roosevelt. His support of Diaz in 1909 resulted in anti-American riots at American owned businesses. Roosevelt ordered 25,000 troops deployed on the Mexican border, and 8,000 Marines deployed with United States Naval exercises in the Gulf of Mexico.

The display of gunboat diplomacy worked. Recognizing the implied threat from the United States, the newly elected Mexican President Francisco Madero ordered a halt to the riots. In response, newly elected governors and mayors suppressed the uprisings.

United States diplomats also took an active role in ending the Moroccan Crisis in 1912. That crisis began with a 1911 revolt in Morocco. The French sent in an army ostensibly to stop the Revolt. However, their actual intent was to add Morocco to their empire. Germany objected and sent a gunboat to the port of Agadir, and later two cruisers. Their pretext was to protect German business interests.

Fearing the establishment of a German treaty port on the Atlantic, which could threaten Gibraltar, Great Britain sent two pre-Dreadnought battleships. The British Prime Minister in a speech at a private gathering threatened war.

The United States ambassador offered to negotiate an equitable settlement. The Treaty of Fez acknowledged the French protectorate of Morocco, which ended that country's independence. In return, Germany gained the southern portion of the French Congo. With that addition to the German colony of Kamerun, Germany achieved a port on the Congo River. The United States gained additional diplomatic recognition for participating in a settlement which prevented a war between Germany, France, and Great Britain.

The reprieve in Mexico was temporary. Madero was an inexperienced politician who had never held office. However, his election as president in October 1911, raised high expectations for positive change. Madero fervently held to his position that Mexico needed real democracy, which included a free press, and the right of labor to organize and strike. The newspapers enjoyed their new-found freedom, and almost immediately, Madero became the target for their criticism.

Naively, Madero ordered rebel leaders who helped him to power to demobilize and return to civilian life. These were men of action, and when promised reforms were not immediately apparent, one by one they rose in revolt. Within months, Mexico was in the throes of civil war.

The Madero presidency was unraveling. In February 1913, Madero dispatched General Victoriano Huerta to combat revolutionaries fighting within Mexico City. In a time known as the *Ten Tragic days*, Huerta sided with the rebels and imprisoned Madero and the Vice President in the Presidential Palace.

The United States Ambassador Henry Lane Wilson brokered the Pact of the Embassy. This agreement formalized the alliance of General Huerta and General Felix Diaz, the nephew of the former president. With the backing of the United States, Huerta became the provisional President. Madero and his vice president resigned and agreed to go into exile. However, on their way to exile, they were murdered by the guards. Hoping for stability, virtually all the nations with embassies in Mexico City immediately recognized Huerta's government.

Chapter 21

The Election of 1912

Roosevelt declined to run for a third term. Instead, he handpicked his Secretary of War William Howard Taft to be his successor. With the progressives in the ascendancy of the Republican Party, they engineered the nomination of the Senator from Wisconsin Robert LaFollette to be Vice President.

The Democrats endured a very contentious convention. On the forty-sixth ballot, with the support of William Jennings Bryan, they nominated the Governor of New Jersey Woodrow Wilson for President. Then they chose Thomas Marshall from New York as the candidate for Vice President.

The Socialists again nominated Eugene Debs

Teddy Roosevelt campaigned hard for the Taft – LaFollette ticket. With his characteristic high-energy campaign style.

He used his *Bully Pulpit* to excoriate Wilson's run for President as the fourth campaign of William Jennings Bryan. An assassination attempt on Roosevelt by a Wilson supporter, John Shrank, on October 14, soured public opinion on Wilson. The bullet struck Roosevelt in the chest. However, Roosevelt's steel eyeglass case deflected the shot into a fifty-page folded copy of his speech. Characteristically, Roosevelt gave his speech before seeking medical attention.

Police arrested the would-be assassin. Shrank was tried and convicted of attempted murder of the President of the United States, and sentenced to hang. Roosevelt, in one of his last acts as President, commuted the sentence to life in prison.

LaFollette also campaigned hard, particularly in big cities and areas populated by union members. Combined, they stumped for Taft in every State.

Taft chose the traditional style of a

candidate for President and campaigned from his front porch. Crowds of voters gathered three or four times per week to hear him speak. He promised a continuation of Roosevelt's policies.

Wilson campaigned on the slogan *A New Freedom*. His policy focused on individualism instead of big government. Like Taft, he mostly campaigned from his home, making speeches from his front porch. William Jennings Bryan stumped the country for Wilson. Often, his rallies competed with those of Roosevelt and LaFollette.

The vote tallies on November 5 provided the Taft – LaFollette ticket 50.7 percent of the vote. Wilson received 41.7 percent, and Eugene Debs received six percent. Minor candidates accounted for the balance of the votes.

The Electoral College provided four-hundred and sixty votes for Taft and LaFollette, and one-hundred and twenty-seven for Wilson and Marshall. The Wilson – Marshall ticket only won the eleven Solid

South states. Wilson received 100,000 fewer votes than William Jennings Bryan received in 1908.

1912 would be the last election when the total number of electoral votes increased with the population. The Apportionship Act of 1911 capped the number of members of the House of Representatives to 473, based on the 1910 Census

If a new state joined the Union in between the di-centennial census, the House would temporarily add one representative per state until the next the census. Thus, the new states of New Mexico and Arizona each elected one representative.

Following future di-centennial census reports, the House would be re-apportioned within the 473 maximum number of members. Each state would have at least one seat in the House of Representatives.

The number of members of the Senate was not capped. According to the Constitution, each state elected two Senators. With the current total of fifty-six states, the total number of 112 Senators would only change with the addition of more states.

Taft's Inauguration took place on March 4, 1913. The day before the inauguration, 8,000 women marched in the first Woman's Suffrage Parade. LaFollette, a strong supporter of woman's suffrage proudly stood on the reviewing stand as his wife Belle Case LaFollette marched at the head of the parade alongside a leading Women's Suffragette and parade organizer Inez Milholland. Both women rode on white horses.

Following the Inauguration ceremonies, Theodore Roosevelt left Washington and returned to his Long Island estate, Sagamore Hills. Within months, the morose former President, frustrated being out of the limelight, needed to separate himself from politics. At his wife, Edith's suggestion, Roosevelt, and Edith were on their way for a year-long hunting trip to Africa.

Chapter 22

President Taft began his administration during an atmosphere of crisis in Europe. The fear of war over the Moroccan Crisis strengthened the Entente between England and France.

Italy declared war on the Ottoman Empire when the Ottomans refused to cede Lybia to the Italians. The Italian Army invaded, and the Italian Navy defeated the small Ottoman squadron stationed in Benghazi. Italy took control of the coast. However, the Ottoman-Arab tribes in the interior thwarted all attempts by the Italians to complete their conquest. With the war stalemated, a brutal guerrilla war followed. The Ottomans agreed to a peace treaty ceding Lybia to Italy when the Balkan Countries attacked Turkish territory in the Balkan Peninsula.

The Ottoman Empire before the First Balkan War

The First Balkan War occurred when the countries including Greece, Bulgaria, Serbia, and Montenegro, took advantage of the Italian – Ottoman War to attack the remnants of the Ottoman Empire located on the Balkan Peninsula. The allies conquered most of the Ottoman territory and pushed the Turks back to the outskirts of Constantinople. A peace brokered by Germany, Austria-Hungary and Italy ended the war, with the allies annexing the territory they occupied and creating Albania as an independent country.

Within months the former allies squabbled over their territorial gains. Bulgaria declared war on her former allies. After initial successes, the Bulgarian's suffered defeats. The Ottoman Empire declared war on Bulgaria and re-gained its territory in Thrace. Romania invaded from the north and took the disputed province of Dobruja.

Surrounded by enemies, Bulgaria sued for peace, losing much of the territory gained in the First Balkan War.

The European powers also formed conflicting alliances. Germany, Austria-Hungary, and Italy formed the Triple Alliance. The United Kingdom, France, and Russia formed the Triple Entente. All the nations expanded their armies and naval forces.

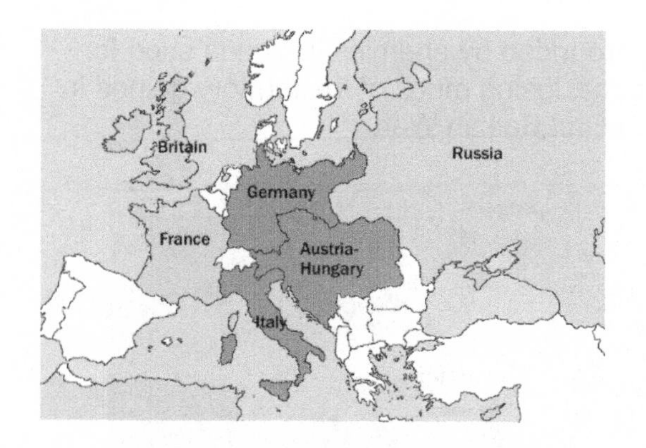

Triple Alliance versus Triple Entente

The Balkan Crisis of 1875, resulted in the Independence of Serbia. During their War of Independence from the Ottoman Empire, Serbia briefly conquered Bosnia. The Congress in Berlin returned the province to the Ottoman Empire but placed it under the protection of Austria-Hungary. Serbia protested as the population consisted predominately of Serbian Orthodox Christians.

In 1908, Austria-Hungary formally annexed Bosnia – Herzegovina, territories they occupied since 1877. Serbia protested, and sought the aid of Russia. However, Russia still recovering from defeat in the Russo-Japanese War, and the Revolution of 1905 was not ready for war.

Tensions grew between Austria-Hungary and Serbia due to Serbia's intelligence services covert aid to Bosnian Serb revolutionaries. In retaliation, Austria cut off Serbian exports through its territory. The export ban delayed the shipment of Serbian goods, damaging Serbia's economy. Landlocked Serbia needed to ship her commodities through less popular ports of call. The primed fuse for war just needed a spark.

That spark occurred on June 24, 1914, when a Bosnian Serb nationalist Gavrial Princip's attempted assassination the Austrian Archduke Francis Ferdinand, the heir to the Austrian throne. The Archduke was on an inspection tour of military preparedness and visited the governor in Sarajevo.

The conspirators stationed six members of

Black Hand a terrorist group, backed by Serbia, along with the published route of travel of the Royal Motorcade. One conspirator threw a grenade, which injured occupants of the fourth car.

The Archduke ordered his car to go to the hospital. His driver took a wrong turn and stalled the engine while backing up. That provided Princip with the opportunity to fire three shots. The first hit the Archduke in the shoulder, the second hit him in the chest, the other hit Sophie in the abdomen. The Archduke, severely wounded, held his wife in his arms as she lay dying, crying out for her not to leave him. The driver rushed the critically injured Archduke to the hospital for treatment, where he stayed for two weeks. Then the government transferred him to Vienna for a 2-month convalescence.

Princip and his five co-conspirators all attempted suicide by swallowing cyanide. However, the pills were defective. Following intensive interrogation sessions, the conspirators implicated Serbian intelligence in the plot. The conspirators were tried, convicted, and all but Princip executed. Princip, being only nineteen, was ineligible for the death penalty. The court sentenced him to twenty-five years in prison.

The Serbian Government surprised by the assassination attempt offered its sincere condolences. Investigations done by Austrian and Serbian investigators concluded that no direct evidence existed indicating involvement by the Serbian government, and to the contrary, most of the evidence exonerated the Serbian government. However, the evidence clearly showed that Serbian intelligence officials actively supported the Black Hand.

The Austrian Government did not need or want proof. With the heir to the throne languishing in the hospital at death's door, and the Grand Dutchess murdered, Austria thirsted for revenge. Backed by Kaiser Whilehm II's guarantee of support, the Austrian government issued a ten-point ultimatum demanding Serbia surrender much of its sovereignty to Austria within 48 hours. Serbia agreed to eight of the demands and offered the others to arbitration. On July 28, the Austrians declared war on Serbia. Soon, the splendid conflict of punishment of Serbia escalated into a world war.

In response to Austria-Hungary's declaration of war on Serbia, Russia declared war on Austria-Hungary. Two days later the German Empire demanded that Russia stop mobilization, and declared war on Russia when the Russians ignored the demand. France then declared war on Germany and Austria-Hungary.

Great Britain undertook diplomatic action to bring the Powers together in a conference. The Crown felt that as mobilization took several weeks, a negotiated settlement was possible. The Entente agreement with France and Russia only included a declaration of war if Germany attacked first. Since both nations independently declared war on Germany, the Entente did not apply. Great Britain did not have such an agreement with Serbia but did have mutual defense agreements with Belgium, Luxembourg, and Holland.

The Taft Administration declared the neutrality of the United States and cooperated with Great Britain's attempts to secure a negotiated settlement. The general view, endorsed by Vice President LaFollette, regarded the war as a European issue. The 3,000 miles wide Atlantic Ocean served as an effective barrier. The mighty United States Navy served as a deterrent within that barrier.

Taft ordered the navy to speed the development of the South Dakota Class of six Super Dreadnoughts. The battleships design characteristics included an overall length of 684 feet, a beam of 106 feet, and a displacement of 43,000 tons. These were the largest warships to date built for the United States Navy. Armaments consisted of four, triple turrets of sixteen-inch guns, two mounted forward and two aft in the superfiring position. Secondary weapons included sixteen, six-inch guns in twin turrets, four turrets per side. The Navy chose shipyards in New York, Mare Island, Newport, Norfolk, and Fore River to construct the battleships simultaneously. The Navy estimated completion time as twenty-four months. The New York shipyard contracts included the USS South Dakota and the USS Indiana. Other warships in the class included: USS Montana, USS Massachusetts, USS Iowa, and USS North Carolina.

Mexico's unrest distracted Taft from the European War. In *The Tampico Affair*. Taft's cordial relations with President Huerta soured when Taft refused to sell Huerta weapons. Mexican authorities arrested nine United States Navy sailors, from the gunboat USS Dolfin who tried to purchase gasoline while on leave. When Mexico refused demands for their release, The battleships USS Florida and USS Utah, plus a transport ship with 500 Marines took the port city Veracruz and held it for six months.

On July 14, President Huerta abdicated and fled into exile. Mexico descended into civil war, which spilled over the United States border from bandits, notably by Pancho Villa. Taft sent the United States Army on punitive raids, to hunt down the bandits. The attacks soon escalated until the United States Army occupied the bordering

Mexican states Sonora and Chihuahua; as most of the bandit raids originated from there. United States Spanish speaking civilian administrators arrived to assist the local Mexican authorities to set up municipal governments, schools, and local police departments.

Within months, with the US Army providing stability, the Mexican citizens felt secure enough to view them as protectors instead of occupiers. The Mexicans began to provide valuable information about the bandit band members and locations. One by one, the bandit bands were captured or killed.

Chapter 23

THE GREAT WAR

The Western Front

On August 3, 1914, Germany launched a massive attack on France, moving its armies through Belgium and Luxenberg. Germany initially asked for safe passage but invaded in force when the Belgians refused. Great Britain exercised its mutual defense pacts with Belgium and declared war on Germany following Germany's refusal to withdraw. The Belgians fought hard, delaying the German advance for two weeks. The remnants of the Belgian army retreated towards Antwerp, hoping for rescue by the Royal Navy.

The Germans paused for reinforcements, then seizing the time it would take for the British to mobilize and move troops into France, pushed hard for Paris. Germany is following the Von Schlieffen Plan to knock the French out of the war before the six-million man Russian Army can mobilize.

Calais, France

August 20, 1914

Major Robert Pomeroy led the Second Batallion of the First Regiment of the Royal Fusiliers from the troopship. His unit was the first troops of 80,000 soldiers of the British Expeditionary Force (BEF) landing at Calais. The Fusiliers, like the rest of the Expeditionary Force, were highly trained professional soldiers. The German 1st Army was rapidly approaching Mons, Belgium, and the British troops rushed to Mons to reinforce the French Fifth Army.

Robert followed his father and grandfather into the British Army. His family, landed squires in Nottingham, had a rich history of military service. The walls at Pomeroy Manor displayed the uniformed paintings of his ancestors. Robert graduated from the Royal Military College at Sandhurst in 1898, which specialized in training young gentlemen cadets in the infantry and cavalry. His first taste of combat was in the Second Boer War in South Africa. He landed in South Africa in January 1900 with

Lord Roberts army. He distinguished himself at the Battle of the Tulega Heights, receiving his promotion from Ensign to Lieutenant. Following the war, his unit transferred to India, where he won his Captaincy. In 1912, he returned to England as an instructor at The Royal Military College. On August 4, 1914, he volunteered for the *BEF* and received a promotion to Major.

On August 22, three battalions of *BEF* troops reached the Canal Du Centre. The canal' position created a salient in the British position. Pomeroy's battalion anchored the left flank, The Middlesex Regiment held the center, and Gordon's Highlanders anchored the right.

Pomeroy positioned Lieutenant Maurice Dease's company to defend the Nimy Bridge, while he protected the Ghiln Bridge. At 6 am the German artillery bombardment began, and the frontal attack stepped off at 9 am. During the first assault, the Germans advanced towards the bridges in columns. At 1,000 yards the British machine guns began firing. As the attackers were in columns, the machine gun fire mowed down the attackers, repulsing the assault with heavy casualties.

After regrouping, the next German assault spread out the attack and moved up their machine guns. British casualties began to mount. Lieutenant Dease's section took heavy casualties, causing him to work the machine gun. After suffering five wounds, Dease died from loss of blood.

Pomeroy ordered his troops to fall back, leaving a rearguard to slow the attack. Those men died where they stood. However, their bravery allowed the rest of the battalion to conduct a fighting retreat.

The Fusiliers sustained over 400 killed or wounded. The Middlesex Regiment and the Highlanders sustained similar casualties and began a fighting withdrawal. That withdrawal became a general retreat when the French Fifth Army collapsed and fled the field. At the last moment, the Royal Ulster Regiment launched a counter-attack, allowing the retreating soldiers to escape into France.

The next two weeks became a nightmare of building defenses, then abandoning them in the face of overwhelming German assaults, which became known as *The Great Retreat*. The battered British 1st Corp and the remnants of the fifth French Army crossed the Marne River on September 2 following a retreat of two-hundred and fifty miles. The previous two weeks of battle resulted in eighty percent casualties.

The *BEF* contemplated retreating to the English Channel ports in preparation for evacuation. The German Army advanced to within ten miles of Paris. Panic reigned in Paris with civilians clogging the roads in a desperate attempt to escape the anticipated carnage.

Unexpectedly, Russia mobilized quickly, and attacked East Prussia, pushing back German defenders. Now fighting a two-front war, Germany moved several divisions by railroads into East Prussia under General Paul Von Hindenburg and Erich Ludendorff. The fresh troops enveloped and virtually annihilated the Russian Army at the Battle of Tannenberg, capturing over 125,000 Russian soldiers. The victorious Germans pursued the retreating remnants of the Russian Army out of East Prussia, deep into the Russian province of Poland. There, the Germans constructed strong fortifications.

Battle of the Marne
September 5 – 12, 1914

On the Western Front, the absence of the German divisions enabled a French observation balloon to detect a gap in the German advance. French General Joffre and the *BEF* seized the opportunity and attacked through the center of the opening and repulsed the Germans. On the western flank, the *BEF* crossed over the Marne, widening the gap between the two German Armies.

To prevent encirclement, the Germans retreated, launching numerous counter-attacks as delaying actions. The counter-attacks allowed the main army to withdraw ninety-miles to the Aisne River. There they dug in on the north side of the river on high ground, destroying the bridges after the entire army crossed over. Situated on the northern plateau, the Germans commanded a wide range of fire.

Robert Pomeroy, newly promoted to Lt. Colonel and the new commander of the Middlesex Regiment, attended the *BEF* senior officer staff meeting to plan the assault on the German position. Optimism filled the room, as following the defeats on the Great Retreat, the allies were now on the offensive.

The bulk of the *BEF* I Corp would cross the Aisne River on pontoon bridges under cover of an artillery barrage. The Middlesex Regiment's assignment was to pass over a pontoon bridge at night under cover of darkness and the expected morning fog.

Once across, Pomeroy's men would work their way up the narrow trails in the escarpments cut in the ridgeline through erosion. The Middlesexers would then attack the German trench fortifications from the flank, and disrupt them with enfilading fire.

At 2-am on September 13, Pomeroy led the Middlesex Regiment over the Aisne River on the pontoon bridge, then cut it adrift so the engineers could haul it back to the British side of the river. That would avoid the potential of discovery by any German patrols. The die was cast. The Middlesexers were on the German side of the river with no way back if the frontal attack did not go off as scheduled.

Quietly, Pomeroy led his men to the base of the escarpment, located the trails, sent out sentries, and ordered his men to rest. The regiment left any unnecessary or noisy equipment and smoked their last cigarettes before crossing the river. They then deposited their cigarettes and lighters into boxes until they returned.

At 7 am the regiment awakened with the start of the artillery barrage. The thick fog obscured vision. The Middlexers ate a cold breakfast then in single file started to walk up the steep escarpment trail. The German artillery responded with counter-battery fire, and the German soldiers huddled in their trenches and fortifications. The pontoon bridges slowly extended across the river.

By 8 am the *BEF* I Corp marched over a dozen temporary bridges as they crossed over the Aisne River. By 9 am, over 10,000 crossed over. The sun was beginning to be visible through the fog. The artillery barrage let up, then started to walk forward. The soldiers followed the barrage, first at a walk then started to run ahead as the German artillery and mortars exploded among them. As they reached the steeply sloping ridgeline, German machine guns began to cut vast swaths through the advancing soldiers.

On the escarpment trail, one-half of Pomeroy's regiment reached the top and began to advance towards the German trenches. Pomeroy was at the top of the path urging his men to hurry when the German machine guns covering the top of the ridgeline began firing from three sides. Realizing his regiment had climbed into a trap, Pomeroy tried to rally his men to flank the machine gun emplacements. His goal changed from enfilading the trenches to extracting his regiment.

Within 30-minutes, over half of the soldiers who crested the ridgeline were casualties. Pomeroy himself sustained wounds in his shoulder and arm. He ordered a retreat in sections, leaving the dead and most of the severely wounded behind. German snipers harassed the regiment as it conducted a fighting retreat down the trail, picking off stragglers and decimating groups. Less than forty percent reached the bottom of the path. By this time, Pomeroy sustained a third wound in the thigh and needed assistance to cross the river.

The frontal assault ended in disaster. None of the attackers reached the German trench line. The *BEF* sustained over forty percent casualties before beginning the retreat, and over fifty percent before re-crossing the river under heavy German artillery fire.

On the eastern flank of the gap, the French Army was unable to assist the *BEF*, as the Germans conducted a counter-offensive towards Verdun, almost investing the city. That offensive caused the French to move the Fifth Army to support the Verdun defenders. The German commander, General Von Moltke, with his goal accomplished, broke off the offensive and marched his army west to link up with the defenders at the Aisne River.

Then the Germans, French and British raced to the sea, in an attempt to turn each others flank, erecting trench lines and fortifications along the way. The Western Front settled into trench warfare. Entrenched soldiers, utilizing machine guns and mortars repulsed massed frontal attacks with heavy casualties. One of these campaigns occurred at Ypres in Belgium from October 19 to November 22.

The battle began on October 19. The German intended to capture Dunkirk and Calais. To accomplish this, the Germans simultaneously attacked the Belgian Army defending the Yser River along a three-mile front, breaking through and crossing the river. The Belgian retreat almost became a rout, which was narrowly averted when King Albert I ordered the sluice gates of the dikes opened, which flooded the plain of Flanders. In danger of having a portion of their army cut off, the Germans retreated behind the rising river. Opening the sluices saved Calais and Dunkirk, and also ended the campaign near the Yser River, as the ground became a sea of mud.

Two days later, the Germans struck the right flank of the *BEF* relief force sent to shore up the Belgian Army. The attack fell heavily on IV Corp. After 2-days of heavy fighting, IV Corp posted urgent radio calls for assistance. I Corp, previously withdrawn from the line for rest and replenishment, responded and advanced towards the sound of gunfire.

Lt. Colonel Pomeroy's Middlesex Regiment joined the Seventh Division of IV Corp in the trenches at Gheluvelt just as the Germans were overwhelming the defenders. Fierce hand to hand fighting erupted using fists, knives, and shovels. Slowly the Germans began to melt away. The counter-attack by the Middlesex stopped the German Advance. Then without forethought, Pomeroy blew his whistle to attack the retreating Germans. With a loud cheer, the Middlesexers continued their counter-attack, moving forward two-hundred yards, then jumped into the vacated German Trench.

The Seventh Division soldiers joined in the charge. Minutes later a heavy German barrage foretold of an impending attack. Pomeroy, realizing his exposed position, ordered a withdrawal back to the original Seventh Division trenches. Combined, the Middlesex Regiment and the remnants of the Seventh Division repulsed the expected German attack. The Germans then re-occupied their previous positions they held before the battle. Thousands of men from both sides died, and not an inch of the ground changed hands.

Reinforcements relieved the Middlesex Regiment and the Seventh Division. The battered troops slogged back to the rear echelon. Morale plummeted. Soldiers with vacant eyes looked at each other with the unasked question – why.

Of the 1,150 officers and men of the Middlesex Regiment who initially marched into France with the *BEF* less than 400 remained. As the combat at Ypres wound down in mid-November, the positions at the beginning of the battle were mostly unchanged.

By the end of 1914, a stalemate existed from Verdun to the English Chanel. In five-months of warfare, over one million soldiers, from both sides are casualties. During the first week of August, 100,000 soldiers of the *BEF* marched into France. On December 31, 95,654 the casualty count reduced the number of active soldiers by 95 percent.

The *BEF*, the best of the professional soldiers in the British Army for all purposes ceased to exist. Lord Kitchener, the Secretary of State, held back three divisions of veterans in case the Germans decided to invade Great Britain. He began a massive volunteer campaign. Over 2,000,000 men volunteered before the institution of the draft.

BRITONS
"WANTS
YOU"
JOIN YOUR COUNTRY'S ARMY!
GOD SAVE THE KING

Chapter 24

Naval Operations

The Imperial German Navy started the war with fourteen Dreadnought battleships, with an additional five under construction. Additionally, the High Seas Fleet contained twenty-two pre-Dreadnoughts. In contrast, the Royal Navy Grand Fleet had twice as many Dreadnought and pre-Dreadnought battleships. For the High Seas Fleet to be victorious, the Grand Fleet needed to be drawn into engagements piecemeal and defeated in detail.

On August 28, a Royal Navy squadron ambushed a German coastal patrol at Heligoland Bliht. The Royal Navy timed their ambush at low tide. The shallow channels, known as The Jade, leading into the significant German Naval base at Wilhelmshaven, would not allow passage of Battle Cruisers and Battleships across the bar at low tide. The German Navy sent in light cruisers piecemeal, and Royal Navy Battlecruisers destroyed three of them.

In response, Kaiser Willhelm ordered a stand-down of the German Navy until they rectified the problem. The Royal Navy victory had the unintended consequence of motivating the Germans to solve a long-known issue. For the next three months, dredges widened and deepened the channels to allow the High Seas Dreadnoughts to enter and exit the Jade at any time. Belatedly, the Royal Navy tried to interdict these operations. However, the Royal Navy destroyers sent to torpedo the dredges faced shore batteries on Heligoland Island, which drove them off.

On August 26, the light cruiser *SMS Madgeberg* ran aground in the Gulf of Finland. Facing capture, the officers tried to destroy the codebooks. Substantial fragments remained and were passed on to British Decrypters. Following two months of decryption, the Royal Navy became able to decode most of the German wireless messages.

At the beginning of the war, the United States Navy requested the acceptance of delegations of officers as observers in both the Royal Navy and the High Seas fleets. One of the officers, Lt. Commander David Evans, was attached to the staff of Admiral Beatty's 1st Battlecruiser Squadron consisting of *HMS Lion, HMS Inflexible, HMS Indomitable, HMS Invincible,* and *HMS Indefatigable.* The Admiral chose the new *HMS Lion* as his flagship. Admiral Jellicoe accepted two others on his staff at Scarpa Flow. These observers had bridge access if accompanied by a Royal Navy officer.

The High Seas Fleet accepted three others and assigned them to the staff of Admiral Ingenohl. In late October, Ingerhol became ill with an abdominal infection and taken to Berlin for treatment. Admiral Reinhard Scheer replaced him.

On November 1, Admiral Scheer assigned two of the United States Navy officers to the battlecruiser squadron commanded by Admiral Hipper. He appointed Commander Robert Treat, the son of the famous retired Admiral to Hipper's flagship SMS Seydlitz and Lt. Commander Robert Orr to *SMS Moltke.*

On November 2, the battlecruisers *SMS Seydlitz*, SMS *Moltke*, SMS *Von der Tann*, the armored cruisers *SMS Blucher*, *SMS Yorck,* and the light cruiser *SMS Stralsund*, left the Jade Estuary and steamed towards the English coast. The mission involved the bombardment of Yarmouth. The attack was a prelude to a larger plan of drawing out a portion of the Grand Fleet into a future battle.

At 6 am, the following morning the flotilla arrived off Yarmouth and bombarded the port. The *SVS Stralsund* laid a minefield. The Royal Navy submarine *D5* sortied out of Yarmouth, struck one of the mines laid by *SMS Stralsund* and sank. At 11 am, Hipper ordered his ships to turn back to German waters.

Upon Hipper's return to German waters, his flotilla encountered heavy fog covering the Heligoland Bliht. Hipper ordered the warships to halt until visibility improved so the fleet could safely navigate the defensive minefields. The armored cruiser *SMS Yorck* made a navigational error struck two mines and quickly sank. A patrol boat the *SMS*

Hagen rescued 127 crew members.

Admiral Scheer decided that another raid on the English coast should be carried out. Scheer's plan involved a bombardment of Greater Scarborough, in hopes of drawing out and destroying a portion of the Grand Fleet.

Shortly after 3 am on December 15, *SMS Seydlitz*, SMS *Moltke*, SMS *Von der Tann*, *SMS Derfflinger, SMS Blucher,* the light cruisers *SMS Kolberg*, SMS *Strassburg*, SMS *Stralsund*, *SMS Graudenz*, and two squadrons of torpedo boats (Destroyers) left the Jade. The ships sailed north past the island of Heligoland; then the warships turned west towards Scarborough. Admiral Hipper, uncomfortable with the new wireless communication, preferred the older style signal flags unless the wireless was required.

Twelve hours after Admiral Hipper left the Jade, Admiral Scheer flew his flag on *SMS Frederich der Grosse* and welcomed aboard the third United States officer Commander Thomas Quelley. The High Seas Fleet, consisting of fourteen Dreadnought battleships, eight pre-Dreadnoughts, and a screening force of two armored cruisers, seven light cruisers, and fifty-four torpedo boats, departed to set the ambush of the Grand Fleet. The orders for the day included strict radio silence. Admiral Scheer also preferred signal flags for all but long-distance communications.

Admiral Scheer's Dreadnought Battleships Leaving Jade

Just after 8 am on December 16, as the morning mist began to lift the Admiral Hipper ordered the squadron to lay mines, and fire on the resort town of Scarborough, hitting the grand hotel, private homes, churches, and the railway station. The targets were three radio towers situated near the buildings.

The battlecruisers moved onward to Whitby where they destroyed the Coast Guard station and accidentally hit the ruins of Whitby Abby. The German squadron then targeted Hartlepool, which contained a small naval base. The three, six-inch guns defending the base opened fire, striking *SMS Seydlitz* without damage and SMS Blucher twice before the German Navy gunfire caused the shore battery crews to take shelter.

Four patrolling Royal Navy Destroyers *HMS Doon, HMS Test, HMS Waverly,* and *HMS Moy* closed to 5,000 yards, fired their torpedoes then withdrew. All the weapons missed. The light cruiser *HMS Patrol* tried to engage, but following three, high caliber hits the Captain ordered her run aground.

During the raid, the German warships' laid over 100 mines. The ships shelling of Hartlepool, Scarborough, and Whitby included more than one thousand shells, killing 112, and wounding 443. Damage included about 300 houses, seven churches, and five hotels. At 9:30 am, Admiral Hipper ordered his warships to close formation, placed the torpedo boats and light cruisers as a forward screen, and set course back to Germany.

Chapter 25

The Battle of Dogger Bank

The Royal Navy decryption experts deciphered much of the German wireless messages but did not know the exact destination. Learning about the High Seas Fleet's bombardment of Scarborough, Admiral Beatty's 1st Battlecruiser Squadron and a squadron of seven destroyers left Cromarty at 06:00 setting course to Dogger Bank. Beatty correctly estimated that the Germans would take the most direct route back to the Jade.

At 11:00 am Admiral Beatty' 1st Battle Cruiser Squadron rendezvoused with Admiral Sir John Warrender's Dreadnought Battleship Squadron. Sir John flew his flag on *HMS King George V.* Her sister ships *HMS Ajax, HMS Orion, HMS Conqueror,* and *HMS Monarch* comprised the rest of the squadron. Additional warships included the First Light Cruiser Squadron consisting of

HMS Southampton, HMS Birmingham, HMS Falmouth, and *HMS Nottingham.*

Sir John, as senior officer assumed overall command. Together he and Beatty positioned their fleets to intercept Hipper's squadron. The Royal Navy, not knowing where the raid would happen, planned to ambush the German fleet as it returned. However, neither Admiral Beatty nor Admiral Warrender had any knowledge of the presence of Admiral Scheer's High Seas Fleet.

At 5:15 am on 16 December, the destroyer *HMS Lynx* sighted the German torpedo boat *SMS 155.* The destroyer squadron went to investigate. A battle ensued with the torpedo boats and light cruisers of the advance screen of Admiral Scheer's fleet. *HMS Lynx* sustained damage to a propeller. *HMS Ambuscade* struck three times, started to take on water, made smoke, and dropped out of the engagement. *SMS Hamburg* engaged *HMS Hardy* which sustained massive damage and caught fire. Just before she exploded, she fired her torpedoes, which missed.

News of the engagement reached Admiral Scheer. The battle then broke off. However, at 06:03 the remaining Royal Navy destroyer, *HMS Shark* sighted five German torpedo boats, fired two torpedoes and withdrew. The torpedo boats radioed a reported the action. Admiral Scheer ordered them to pursue.

Excitement grew on the bridge of *SMS Frederich der Grosse*. Could this be the engagement the High Seas Fleet so desired? The opportunity to destroy a portion of the Royal Navy's Grand Fleet, and equalize the size of their navies could be on hand.

Radio traffic between the flagship and the battleships ordered the warships to battle stations. The extent of radio traffic also concerned Admiral Jellicoe, the commander of the Grand Fleet. He realized his forces were in jeopardy, and ordered sixteen more

Dreadnoughts to put to sea. However, thick fog at Scarpa Flow delayed their departure for over two hours. At 9:00 am, aboard *HMS Iron Duke* Jellicoe led the Grand Fleet out of Scapa Flow.

The size and construction of the Royal Navy Dreadnoughts and those of the High Seas Fleet were significantly different.
The Royal Navy warships had a worldwide mission to protect the empire. Therefore they were larger to provided living quarters for crew for long journeys, had bigger guns, and were more lightly armored. The focus was on long-range gunnery and speed. Additionally, as the warships were continuously at sea, significant port time was required for repairs and re-supply.

The design of the High Seas Fleet Dreadnoughts accounted for short missions within the North Sea and the Baltic Sea. They were smaller, more heavily armored, had more watertight compartments in the hull, and lower caliber eleven and twelve-inch guns. Crew quarters were more compact as mostly they would be sleeping in harbor barracks.

At 11 am on December 16, Admiral Hipper's advance screen entered Dogger Bank from the west, as Admiral Sheer and the High Seas Fleet came from the southeast. Visibility suddenly improved and Hipper's screening torpedo boats suddenly encountered Admiral Beatty's destroyers. A wild melee ensued with gunfire and torpedoes fired wildly.

On the bridge of *HMS Lion,* Admiral Beatty exulted with the springing of the trap of Admiral Hipper's squadron. Signals flashed between the *HMS Lion, HMS Inflexible, HMS Indomitable, HMS Invincible,* and *HMS Indefatigable* to form a line of battle to intercept the Germans. Radio contact between Admirals Beatty and Sir John Warrender aboard *HMS King George V* confirmed that the faster battlecruisers would take the lead. Beatty invited Lt.

Commander David Evans to the bridge to observe the battle.

Admiral Hipper used his radio to send a coded message to Admiral Scheer advising that he was engaging a Royal Navy battle group at Dogger Bank. Scheer's reply came back that the trap was sprung. The Admiralty in London intercepted both German transmissions. At 11:40, the decoders rushed into the Admiralty, indicating there might be a problem. The Germans were talking about a trap.

The First Lord snorted: "Of course the Germans are talking about a trap, we have Admiral Hipper trapped, and his squadron is about to be destroyed." The decoders tried to demur, but the First Lord turned his back and walked away.

At 11:45 am, a frantic radio message came in from aerial reconnaissance over Wilhelmshaven. The plane's radioman, shouting in the middle of a dogfight reported that the anchorage was empty. With the sound of machine gunfire in the background, he exclaimed, I repeat the anchorage is......

With a stricken look on his face, the First Lord shouted: “Get a wireless message to Admiral Beatty, tell him he is steaming into a trap.” Minutes later, the wireless operator handed the First Lord the microphone. Beatty was on the line with cannon fire in the background saying “With all due respect My Lord, tell me something I don’t already know like where the hell is Admiral Jellicoe.”

HMS Lion steamed in the third position of his line of battle. *HMS Invincible led the column followed by HMS Indefatigable,* with *HMS Inflexible* and *HMS Indomitable* **f**ollowing to the rear, with one mile between each battlecruiser. Six miles to the west, cutting the 1st Battlecruiser Squadron off from escaping towards England steamed Admiral Hipper’s battlecruisers *SMS Seydlitz*, SMS *Moltke*, *SMS Von der Tann*, followed by the armored cruisers *SMS Blucher*, and *SMS Yorck.*

Usually, that would be an advantage to the Royal Navy. However, the High Seas Fleet maneuvered to form envelopment battle lines to the north and south. A Nassau Class Dreadnought and four pre-Dreadnought battleships served as blocking forces on the north and south. Radio transmissions from Admiral Sir John Warrender indicated that Admiral Scheer's Kaiser Class, Helgoland Class, and Nassau class Dreadnoughts outnumbered him 2 – 1, and closed the bottle from the east.

At 12:30 pm, Admiral Jellicoe's fleet steamed at the flank speed of 22 knots towards Dogger Bank, but the distance to the engagement was at least 50 miles. Upon leaving Scarpa Flow, he ordered his three battlecruisers *HMS Queen Mary, HMS New Zealand,* and *HMS Princess Royal* to steam ahead. With their speed of 27.5 knots, they would arrive at Dogger Bank an hour before the battleships.

HMS Invincible, previously struck seven times from fire from *SMS Von der Tann*, *SMS Blucher*, and *SMS Yorck* sustained two hits on Q turret. Flames shot up into the air, then suddenly *HMS Invincible* exploded and broke in half. *HMS Indefatigable*, the next in line, came under concentrated fire. Two shells hit P Turret, penetrated the roof, and exploded inside, killing the gun crew and started quickly spreading fires. Minutes later, she also blew up when the flames reached the magazine.

HMS Lion took several hits below the waterline flooding the port engine room, causing that engine to shut down. Reduced to fifteen knots, *HMS Lion* fell out of the battle line, listing to port. Counter-flooding corrected the list, but the influx of water slowed her to ten knots. More hits registered as her speed slowed. Admiral Beatty transferred his flag to *HMS Southampton*, then to *HMS Indomitable*. He offered to take Lt. Commander Evans with him. Evans initially refused as he was assisting with damage control, but relented when Beatty insisted.

Three German torpedo boats attacked *HMS Lion.* Sustaining heavy fire, two of the torpedo boats sank. The third, *SMS V5* launched four torpedoes striking *Lion's* port side with three. With only one engine functioning, the electric generators failed.

The pumps were unable to contain the flooding.

The order to abandon ship sounded and lifeboats and rafts went over the side. 350 officers and sailors made it to the boats, hundreds of others clung to debris. *HMS Lion's* list increased, and she slowly rolled over, remaining bottom up for several minutes. However, following internal explosions, *HMS Lion* disappeared under the waves.

Admiral Hipper's battlecruisers and armored cruisers also suffered in the battle. Hippers flagship *SMS Seydilitz* sustained fourteen high caliber hits, one of which struck between the two superfiring rear turrets. The explosion and fires knocked both of the gun emplacements out of action.

Seydilitz narrowly escaped destruction when the spreading fire threatened a magazine. Alert damage control officers flooded the magazine. However, 159 seamen, trapped in the turrets, corridors, and magazines perished. SMS *Moltke*, and *SMS Von der Tann* each sustained three hits. *SMS Blucher* and *SMS Yorck* each suffered two hits.

Admiral Beatty decided to break out of the trap. *SMS Seydilitz,* severely damage was mostly out of the fight. SMS *Moltke* and *SMS Von der Tann* were two miles to starboard, and turning around, which would take time. He ordered *HMS Inflexible* and *HMS Indomitable* to charge in line abreast directly at the armored cruisers *SMS Blucher*, and *SMS Yorck.*

HMS Indomitable

Each battlecruiser featured the forward turret and two wing turrets. With twin twelve-inch guns, the wing turrets could face forward or the rear. Beatty ordered full speed ahead. *HMS Indomitable targeted SMS Blucher,* while *HMS Inflexible* targeted *SMS Yorck.* The plan was for both *HMS Inflexible* and *HMS Indomitable* to aim the wing turrets to the front as they charged, then rotate those turrets to fire back as they passed. The battlecruisers could blast their way through and then punish the German cruisers once past without losing forward speed.

SMS Blucher and SMS Yorck, armed with eight-inch guns were unable to prevent Beatty's charging Dreadnought's breakout; and in return, each sustained five high-caliber hits. *SMS Moltke and SMS Von der Tann* also fired at, then pursued *HMS Inflexible* and *HMS Indomitable.* However, the Royal Navy warships were faster, over four miles away, and increasing their lead. *Moltke and Von der Tann* broke off the pursuit and went to the aid of *Blucher,*

Yorck, and *Seydlitz.* Admiral Scheer ordered Admiral Hipper to take his damaged warships home. He also ordered the southern blocking squadron to link up with the main fleet.

Admiral Sir John Warrender's Battleship Squadron consisting of the Dreadnought battleships HMS *King George V, HMS Ajax, HMS Orion, HMS Conqueror,* and *HMS Monarch;* faced overwhelming odds. His fleet was outnumbered two to one by Admiral Scheer's battleships.

Constructed between 1910 and 1912 the King George V Class battleships were similar in size and armament to the German Kaiser Class Dreadnoughts.

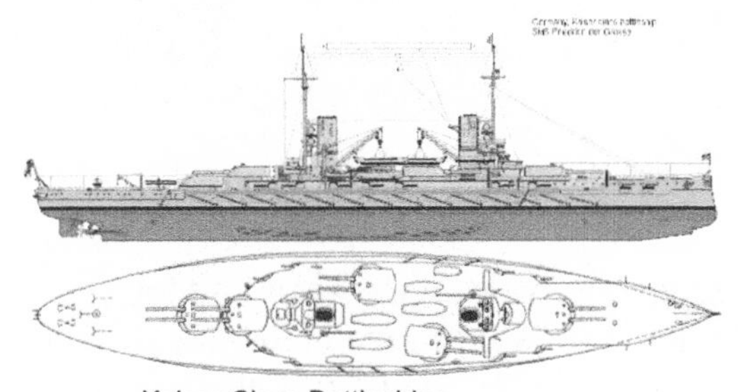

Kaiser Class Battleships

Both battleship classes had five turrets with twelve-inch guns. The Kaiser Class featured centerline turrets fore and aft, with offset wing turrets starboard and port. The rear turrets were in superfiring configuration.

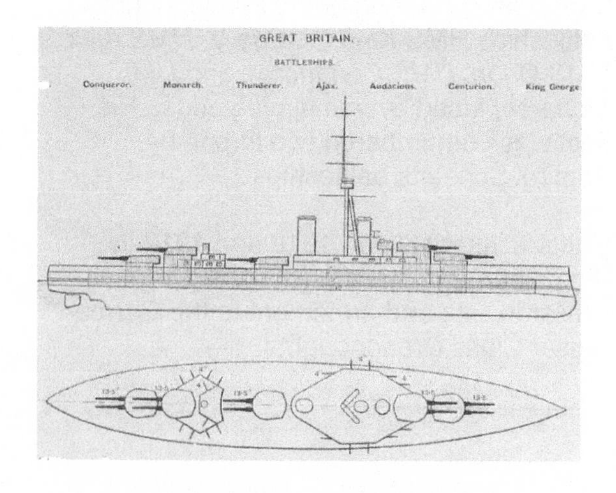

King George V Class Battleships

The King George V Class each had four centerline turrets arranged in the superfiring configuration, with the Q turret amidships.

Admiral Scheer also had six other Dreadnought battleships, four Helgoland Class including *SMS Helgoland, SMS Oldenburg, SMS Ostfriesland* and *SMS Thüringen.* There were two Nassau Class, including *SMS Posen and SMS Westfalen.* The last two were the oldest Dreadnoughts in the fleet, constructed in 1907. The Helgoland's were a more significant and better-armed upgrade of the Nassau design.

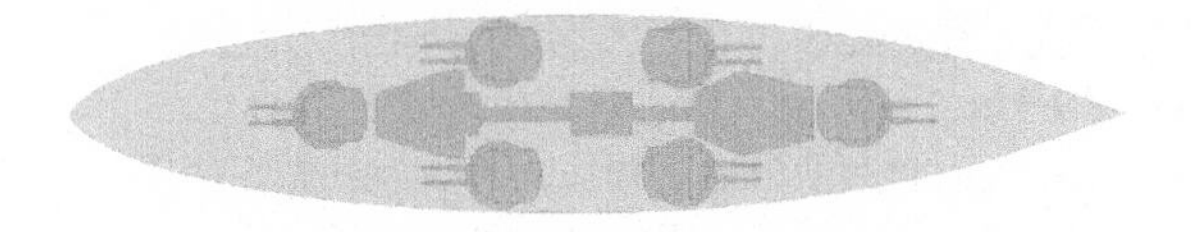

Turret configuration of Helgoland and Nassau Class

Admiral Warrender had a reputation for competency with ships under his command, receiving high marks for accuracy. However, each of his battleships was in combat with two German dreadnaughts of the same time.

By 1 pm, *HMS Ajax, HMS Orion, HMS Conqueror* were burning wrecks, with their crews abandoning ship. On the German side, Royal Navy gunnery sank SMS Posen and severely damaged *SMS Westfalen*. Light cruisers, destroyers, and torpedo boats zeroed in on the damaged Dreadnoughts launching torpedoes at the damaged warships while also firing on each other.

Warrender' flagship, *HMS King George V* dueled with two Kaiser Class Battleships, Admiral Scheer's flagship *SMS Frederich Der Grosse* and *SMS Konig Albert*. *HMS Monarch* dueled with *SMS Kaiserin* and *SMS Prinzregent*. The Helgoland Class battleships including *SNS Helgoland, SMS Oldenburg, SMS Ostfriesland* and *SMS Thüringen* also added the weight of their twelve-inch guns at the two remaining Royal Navy battleships as the German Dreadnoughts closed to within one-mile.

Four shells hit *HMS King George V* simultaneously penetrating both A and B turrets. Second later, magazine explosions blew her up in a ball of fire.
HMS Monarch sustained a dozen hits, became a burning wreck, and began to settle by the bow. Two shells struck the

bridge, killing the captain and the command staff. The executive officer, stationed in the secondary bridge gave the order to abandon ship. As lifeboats and rafts went over the side, the German Dreadnoughts ceased fire and lowered boats to assist in the recovery survivors. Thirty minutes later, *HMS Monarch's* bow slipped beneath the waves. Her stern raised in the air, and with an explosive venting of air and steam, she knifed beneath the waves.

HMS Queen Mary, HMS New Zealand, and *HMS Princess Royal* encountered the escaping *HMS Inflexible* and *HMS Indomitable.* Admiral Beatty, the senior officer, took command and the five battlecruisers and set course for Dogger Bank. Thirty minutes later, lookouts reported eight Royal Navy light cruisers and destroyers steaming away from the battle. Signal flags indicated they were the few survivors of the fight. Admiral Beatty received the wireless message from the largest escaping warship *HMS Southampton.* Her captain reported the destruction of Admiral Warrender's battleship squadron. Beatty ordered the remaining light cruisers and destroyers to form up with the battlecruisers.

Admiral Beatty ordered his fleet to Dogger Bank to look for any survivors. Debris and oil slicks indicated areas of the most ferocious fighting. The cold water claimed its victims. There were no signs of survivors or the German warships, which retreated back to German waters. Beatty ordered the fleet to steam to Scapa Flow. Within an hour, Admiral Jellicoe's Grand Fleet arrived. Following a brief meeting, the combined fleet steamed to Scapa Flow.

Chapter 26

Dogger Bank Aftermath.

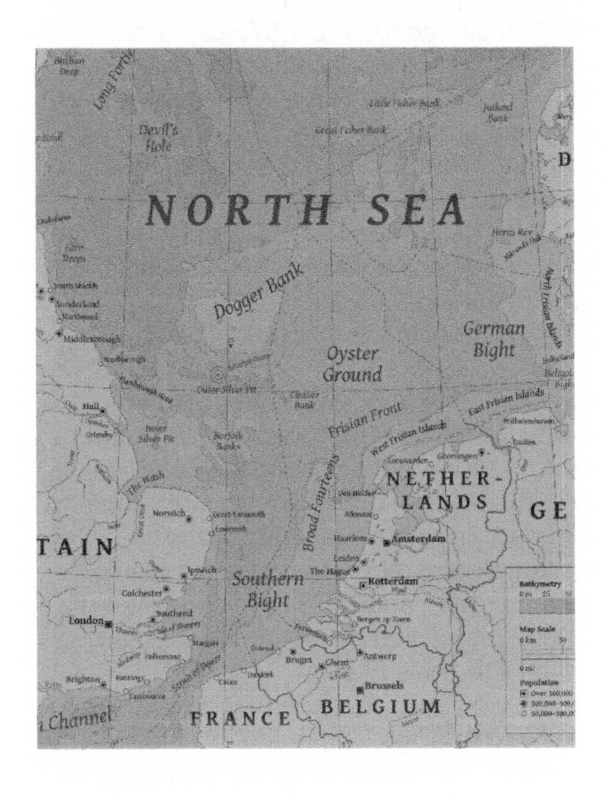

Dogger Bank was the worst defeat in the history of the modern Royal Navy. The High Seas Fleet sank eight Dreadnoughts while losing only one. Casualties included 6,551 British dead, and 1,875 captured. The German losses included 457 killed and 375 wounded. The Royal Navy's advantage in Dreadnoughts of 28 to 17 decreased to 19 to 16. Another King George V Class battleship, *HMS Audacious,* struck a mine and sank before the battle. The Royal Navy operations became cautious until the commissioning of replacement Dreadnoughts in the summer of 1915.

The court of inquiry exonerated Admiral Beatty from blame for the defeat at Dogger Bank. The court held Sir John Warrender, presumed lost with his flagship *HMS King George V* accountable for the debacle. Admiral Beatty received praise for saving *HMS Inflexible* and *HMS Indomitable* from certain destruction by the unexpected arrival of the High Seas Fleet.

The German High Command exulted over the victory. The loss of *SMS Posen*, one of their smaller battleships, became viewed as an acceptable price to pay for a triumphant success. High Command paid little concern to the fact that the Royal Navy Dreadnoughts were conveniently positioned to intercept Admiral Hippers squadron. After all, the total focus of the operations was to lure a portion of the Grand Fleet to destruction.

The survival of *SMS Seydlitz,* and *SMS Westfalen,* both struck by fourteen high-caliber hits vindicated the view that ship to ship, the German Navy had better warships
.

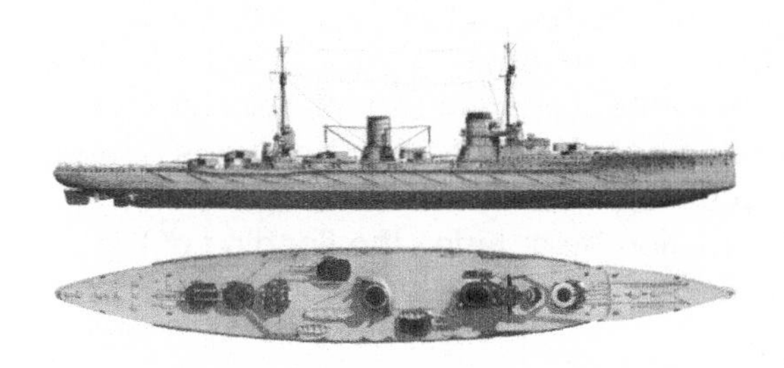

SMS Seydlitz

Damage control officers from *SMS Seydlitz* reported design flaws between the propellant chamber in the barbettes and exits leading to the turrets. One 13.5 inch shell from HMS Lion penetrated the deck and exploded at the rear barbette of the superfiring turrets. The explosion flashed through an open door into the propellant chamber, igniting the charges.

The flames rose high up into the turret and down into the ammunition chamber, then through a connecting door, usually kept shut. However, seamen from the ammunition chamber opened the door in an attempt to escape into the aft turret. That allowed flames to flash through to the other ammunition chamber and up to the second turret. The entire gun crews of both emplacements perished very quickly. The fires rose thirty-feet above the turrets. The Executive officer saved the ship from destruction by ordering the flooding of the magazines.

Corrective action included rerouting the direct passages from the propellant and ammunition chambers to the turrets. The redesign included the installation of more auto-closing fireproof doors to protect the elevators raising propellant and shells into the turrets. The repairs and design changes took three months to complete. *SMS Seydlitz* rejoined the fleet on March 15, 1915. *SMS Westfalen, SMS Blucher, and SMS Yorck* rejoined the fleet a month earlier.

The United States Navy officers returned home in time for the Christmas Holiday celebrations. Through diplomatic channels, Admiral Hipper gave Commander Robert Treat a letter of commendation for bravery under fire. Admiral Beatty provided a similar missive to Lt. Commander David Evans.

All the officers received thirty-day leave, then resumed their posts at the Naval War College in mid-January, 1915. Their reports and evaluations of the performance of the Grand Fleet and the High Seas Fleet were valuable additions in the process of developing new tactics for naval combat.

They all reported the careless handling of shells and propellant by the Royal Navy, which emphasized the rate of fire over safety. That practice allowed for the storing of the powder bags in ordinary closets, and the stacking of them in corridors leading to the gun turrets. They speculated that the careless handling of the explosives was the likely cause of the explosions which destroyed four of the Royal Navy Dreadnoughts.

The design issues involving the turrets, which almost led to the destruction of *SMS Seydlitz* became a hot topic. Lt. Commander Evans confirmed that most of the same conditions existed on the Royal Navy Dreadnoughts.

The officers recommended a thorough review of the United States Navy Dreadnoughts. The new South Dakota Class battleships needed to incorporate changing the hatch mechanisms to open outward instead of inward. This would allow the hatch to be closed and dogged more efficiently. That arrangement would also prevent the spread of fire or water from reaching the rest of the ship. It would also condemn the seamen trapped behind the doors to death. However, the goal was to preserve the warship. The existing battleships would retrofit the new design when next in port.

At Annapolis, in recognition for distinguished service at Dogger Bank and the Naval War College, Commanders Thomas Quelley, David Evans and Robert Treat are appointed as Executive Officers of South Dakota Battleships. Commander Evans assigned to USS South Dakota; Commander Treat assigned to the USS Massachusetts and Commander Quelley to USS North Carolina. Lt. Commander Orr was promoted to Commander and appointed to assume command of the Protected Cruiser USS Chattanooga. The four friends and their wives attend a celebratory dinner before leaving to their new assignments.

Chapter 27

With the beginning of 1915 word reached Berlin that the allies captured all of Germany's possessions in Pacifica. On August 23, 1914, the Japanese, honoring their treaty with Great Britain, declared war on Germany. On August 30 the Japanese landed troops in China and attacked the German Naval Base at Tsingtao. By the end of September, the Japanese captured the base.

In October, a combined Australian and New Zeland naval forces captured German Samoa, German New Guinea, the Bismark Islands, and Nauru. Later, the Japanese navy seized the German colonies in the Marshall and Caroline Islands.

German colonies in Africa came under assault. The Royal Navy prevented Germany from providing support. The Germans understood that nothing could be done to change that situation.

The German Foreign Minister Gottlieb von

Jagow's diplomatic response to the loss of their Pacifica and African colonies was to propose the Nordic Union. This plan would foster a Swedish dominated union between Sweden, Norway, and Denmark. The three nations previously declared their neutrality in August 2014. King Gustav V of Sweden and his Foreign Secretary, Knut Wallenberg were receptive to the plan. However, Prime Minister Hjalmar Hammarskjold demurred as such a union was not possible without a causus belli from Great Britain.

Von Jagow understood but quietly kept up the pressure. Separately, Denmark and Sweden agreed to mine the three narrow straights which permitted access from the North Sea to the Baltic Sea. The Danes mined Storebaelt and Lillebaelt. The Swedish mined Oresund. The mining effectively prevented the Royal Navy's access to the Baltic Sea.

The British Foreign Office could accept the mining, due to the proximity of Denmark and Sweden to Germany. Diplomatically, Britain actively tried to separate Norway from its Scandinavian neighbors. After all, Norway only secured its independence from Sweden in 1905.

British efforts met with resistance. Even though Norwegian sympathies lay with Great Britain, extensive inter-county trade linked the economies of Norway, Sweden, and Denmark. Separation would bring severe economic disadvantages to Norway with little benefit in return.

On May 1, German diplomats attending a banquet in Spain leaked the plans for the Nordic Union. When the news broke, Great Britain demanded Norway, Sweden, and Denmark reject such a union. The three nations denied such a union existed, but could not deny the existence of negotiations to create that union.

The Royal Navy responded by occupying the Norwegian port of Narvik with a garrison of several thousand Royal Marines. Ostensibly, this action secured the Royal Navy's convoy route to Murmansk, Russia. However, the strategic location of Narvik, at the head of the Ofot Fjord, provided the Royal Navy with deep water, ice-free port.

That fact alone dominated the decision to justify the occupation

Sweden, Denmark, and Norway demanded a British withdrawal. When Britain refused, the Swedish Prime Minister, Hammarskjold withdrew his opposition to the creation of the Nordic Union. The Union announced armed neutrality and banned imports and exports to Great Britain while maintaining diplomatic relations.

Diplomatically, the ambassadors of all three countries tried to get the United States to negotiate a settlement with Great Britain. President Taft assigned Secretary of State Philander Chase Knox to conduct the negotiations. Knox was no regular political appointee. He professionalized the diplomatic services and tightly controlled U.S. foreign policy. Knox extended the merit system of selection and promotion from the Consular Service to the Diplomatic Service. He pursued an aggressive role in encouraging and protecting U.S. investments abroad.

On June 15, Knox invited the British

Ambassador and the Ambassadors from Denmark, Norway, and Sweden to the Resort Hotel in Bretton Woods, NH. Attendees at the first banquet included the Governor, Rolland Spaulding, The United States Ambassador to Norway Lantis Swenson, Congressman Cyrus Adams, Congressman Raymond Stevens, and the two United States Senators Henry Hollis and Jacob Gallinger. Local dignitaries and their wives also attended to get a taste of foreign diplomacy.

Before negotiations could begin, positions had hardened. Initially, the residents of Narvik treated British Royal Marines as a curiosity. However, incidents between the locals and the Marines escalated into protest riots, which the Marines suppressed, causing numerous casualties. Soon armed snipers began shooting at sentries. The Marines responded with aggressive patrols and burned the farms of suspected snipers. Norwegian Army units then moved into defensive positions cutting off access to Narvik other than by sea. The presence of the Army prevented further sniper attacks. However, the initial curiosity was now seething resentment, and the initial Norwegian goodwill towards Great Britain evaporated.

Bi-lateral negotiations began on June 16. During opening statements, Norway's Ambassador demanded an unconditional British withdrawal, calling it an invasion. The British Ambassador, Sir Cecil Spring-Rice, rejected the demand, indicating the occupation was temporary, and only to protect the United Kingdom's convoy routes to Russia. He asserted that the United Kingdom did not have territorial designs on any Norwegian territory.

The Swedish and Danish ambassadors stood firmly with Norway. Ambassador Lantis shuttled between the delegations attempting to secure a time frame for British withdrawal. Secretary of State Knox invited Sir Cecil to a private lunch. There he outlined the disadvantages to the Crown due to their occupation of Narvik. Knox began:

"Sir Cecil, the non-belligerent world views your occupation of Narvik as an invasion of a non-aligned country. I understand the Crown's view is that the Nordic Union precipitated your actions. However, the facts of the matter demonstrate otherwise. The union consummated itself following what they term as an invasion, and the Crown's refusal to withdraw.

In the United States, public opinion views Great Britain as the aggressor, and the Norwegian people as the victims. Newspaper editorials are moving towards, and possibly leading that public opinion. The reality is there is little likelihood that the High Seas Fleet would be capable of challenging the Royal Navy's dominance in the North Sea. Submarines can and do breakthrough. However, that is not enough to justify your actions."

Sic Cecil replied: "The High Seas Fleet has demonstrated the capability for offensive actions. We swallowed a bitter pill at Dogger Bank. Do I take from your comments that the United States is siding with the Nordic Block"? Secretary Knox stated:

"Not at all. I am merely commenting on the public opinion of non-aligned states; and the switch in public opinion in the United States, which previously favored the allies. I do not equate Germany's actions in Belgium with the Royal Marines actions in Narvik. However, the newspaper stories and editorials are beginning to lean in that direction. If the Crown wants to retrieve the situation, the time for compromise is now."

Sir Cecil harrumphed then asked: "What is the position of the United States in this war? More importantly, what plans does your administration have moving forward"? Knox replied.

"The answer to both questions is the same. We have no abiding interest in the outcome of your war; which is a European issue and should be settled one way or the other by the European powers. The winners and losers will still have the 3,000 miles wide the Atlantic Ocean separating us, and the United States Navy will enforce that barrier. We will not tolerate the war spreading into North America. However, our diplomatic services are available if a negotiated settlement is deemed to be desirable."

The conversation then turned to personal matters, and shortly the lunch meeting ended. Sir Cecil asked: "Secretary Knox will you share our conversation with the ambassadors from Norway, Sweden, and Denmark." Knox replied.

"Only in general terms, not in substance. I could not be a fair arbitrator if either side felt I favored one side or the other." With that, both men drove off in separate cars. On June 26, with little substantive agreement, the conference adjourned, and the diplomats returned to Washington DC to cable their respective governments, and to receive directives.

On June 28, Secretary Knox met with President Taft and the Cabinet. Taft expressed his disappointment with the lack of progress. He hoped the British would be more amenable to compromise, as for the moment they held the stronger hand. Even if the Nordic Block nations declared war on the United Kingdom, combined, they could do little to alter the balance of power on the continent.

The Secretary of the Navy, George von L. Meyer asked to be recognized. President Taft nodded, and Secretary Meyer stated:

"Mr. President, I am concerned that the Royal Navy will try to occupy Greenland's port city of Godthab and appropriate Greenland from the Danes. I realize that Greenland does not have significant strategic value to the British. However, Greenland could be used as a bargaining chip to put pressure on Denmark. It will also bring the specter of war into North America."

President Taft asked Secretary Knox if during the negotiations the Danish Ambassador Olaf Hastrup voiced concerns. Knox replied: "The topic did not arise, as we were dealing with the occupation of Narvik. However, I will inquire about his concerns, and if Denmark might need our assistance."

The next day, Knox invited Ambassador Hastrup for lunch. During the meeting,

Knox stated: “Mr. Ambassador, the Secretary of the Navy raised concerns that the Royal Navy may attempt to occupy Greenland as a bargaining chip in negotiations. Let me assure you that the United States will not tolerate an occupation of Greenland.”

After a pause, Knox continued: “Denmark is neutral, and so are we. The United States will not allow the war to intrude on North America and is prepared to guarantee the sovereign Danish authority over Greenland. All your government needs to do is make a formal request.”

On July 7, Ambassador Hastrup requested a meeting with Knox. He brought two letters. The first asked that the United States act as the protector of Danish authority in Greenland. The second letter directed to the Royal Inspector of Greenland Carl Frederick Harries instructing him to cooperate with the United States Navy to preserve Danish sovereignty over Greenland.

On July 20, a battle group including the

USS Connecticut, three destroyers, and a transport ship anchored in Godthab. The transport contained two companies of United States Marines, construction materials to erect housing, and supplies for 180-days. The same day, during a news conference with Secretary of State Knox, the Danish Ambassador Olaf Hastrup announced the request by the Danish government for a United States protectorate to preserve Danish sovereignty over Greenland. American military forces protecting Greenland also sent a strong message to the British that the United States would forcibly object to any attempt to bring the war to North America.

Chapter 28

Over the next two years, trench warfare reigned supreme on the Western Front. The allies and the Germans launched numerous attacks and counter-attacks, resulting in over four million casualties. However, all the action did not move the front lines. The trenches provided a war of attrition which favored the defense.

In 1916 the British introduced tanks in an attempt to break the deadlock at Somme. After advances of 2 miles, the tanks became bogged down in thick mud. The Germans use their mobile 37mm field pieces as anti-tank guns.

Remnants of three light artillery platoons, led by Corporal Adolph Hitler destroyed the ten-tank spearhead of the thinly armored tanks. The tanks were slow, averaging three to five miles-per-hour over the muddy battlefield, and became easy targets. Machine gunners pinned down the British infantry. German reinforcements arrive and drive the British infantry out of the German trenches, recovering all the lost ground. Corporal Hitler is killed in the final moments of the counter-attack. He is posthumously promoted to sergeant, and his family received his Iron Cross.

With millions of men serving in the armies, only the very young, elderly, the infirm, and women are available to work. The economies of England, France, Germany, and Austria-Hungary were grinding to a halt. Rationing was everywhere, and shortages of essential commodities, including coal for heat, flour for bread, and fresh meat, keep growing. Civilians wait in long lines for the products, often only to find empty shelves. Discontent with political leadership is beginning to develop.

On the Eastern Front, the Germans repulsed a Russian offensive. The counter-offensive broke through the retreating Russian Army. The Germans captured Warsaw and kept moving east along a broad front from the Baltic Sea coast to Ukraine. With the front lines on the outskirts of Riga, the German Army's guns brought the Russian Navy base in Riga within range, resulting in the abandonment of the seaport.

When the offensive finally halted to re-supply, the combined German and Austro-Hungarian armies recovered the territory gained by the Russians in Austria-Hungary. The German Army occupied all of the Russian provinces of Poland, Lithuania, and the coast of Latvia.

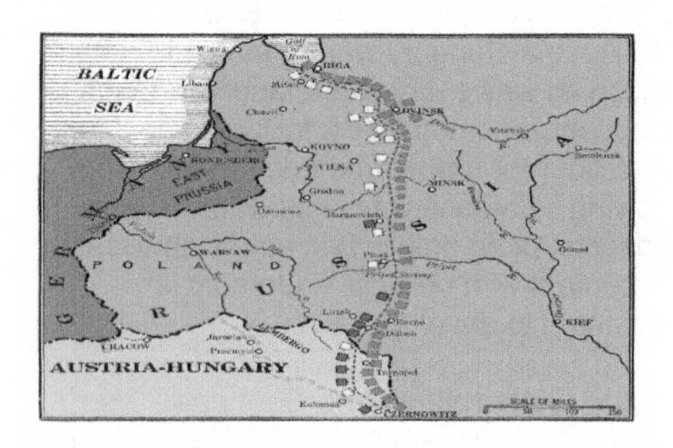

With the threat from Russia significantly reduced, Austria-Hungary and Germany turned their attention to Serbia. In a two month offensive, the invaders repeatedly defeated the combined Serbian and

Montenegro Army, driving it into Albania. The Albanians resisted, inflicting thousands of additional casualties. The Serbian retreat reached Albania's Capital Tirana. There the Italian and Royal Navy's rescued the remnants, transporting them to several Greek Isles in the Aegean Sea.

In Russia, chaos abounded. Russian armies suffered enormous defeats with over 7,000,000 casualties including dead, wounded and missing. Desertion rates averaged almost 34,000 per month. Refugees from German-controlled Poland, Lithuania, and the coast of Latvia fleeing to the east strained the economies, and famine loomed. The inefficiently operated railroad systems collapsed under the strain of military demands, and civilian needs.

The Battle of Jutland

Admiral Scheer attempts to lure the Royal Navy into a battle similar to Dogger Bank. Unknown to him, British Intelligence is reading his orders in real-time, and bait a trap of their own in the North Sea off the Danish Jutland Peninsula.

Admiral Beatty, aboard his flagship *HMS Princess Royal* led the First Battlecruiser Squadron including *HMS Queen Mary, HMS Tiger*, *HMS Inflexible* and *HMS Indomitable* to attack High Seas Fleet battlecruisers commanded by Admiral Hipper, aboard his flagship *SMS Seydlitz*. Hippers squadron also included *SMS Von der Tan, SMS Moltke, SMS Derflinger, and SMS Goeben*. According to plan, Hipper's warships engage Beatty's squadron, then retreat towards the main battle line of the High Seas Fleet. Knowing the German battle plan, Beatty pursues but abruptly withdrew upon the destruction of the *HMS Indomitable*.

Both of these battlecruisers sustained several twelve-inch hits from *SMS Von der Tan, and SMS Derflinger,* two in Q Turret. The Royal Navy did not have the benefit of hindsight from the Battle of Dogger Bank. There, flooding the magazines saved *SMS Seytlitz* from destruction by fires, caused by poor handling of explosives. *HMS Indomitable* blew up spectacularly.

During the retreat, *HMS Inflexible* struck in the same manner also blew up. Admiral Beatty uttered the memorable words: "There is something wrong with our ships today." HMS *Princess Royal* struck, in the same manner, is saved when an alert officer orders the flooding of the magazine.

In hot pursuit, the German High Seas Fleet is lured northward towards the advancing Grand Fleet commanded by Admiral Jellicoe. His warships cross the High Seas Fleet "T" blasting away at the German forward ships.

Admiral Scheer orders a parallel course and the two fleets' fire furiously at each other. The High Seas Fleet is better armored, but the total weight of shot from the Royal Navy warships is unmistakable. Realizing the more massive British fleet outguns him, Scheer disengages by abruptly turning away using the night as cover. Recognizing that the moment is past, Admiral Jellicoe does not risk a pursuit into German minefields and instead orders the Royal Navy to head home to Scapa Flow.

Both sides claimed victory. The Germans sank 14 of the 151 British ships, including four Dreadnoughts. The High Seas Fleet lost 11 of 99 warships, including one Dreadnought, with three severely damaged.

SMS Seytlitz, hit twenty-four times barely makes it back to Wilhelmshaven. Only the superior construction and multiple watertight compartments saved her from sinking. She was in dry dock four months during repairs.

SMS Seydlitz returning to Wilhelmshaven after the Battle of Jutland

In reality, both claims are correct. The High Seas Fleet won a tactical victory. However, strategically, the Royal Navy retains its dominance of the North Sea, and the naval blockade of Germany remains intact. More importantly, from the after-action reports from *HMS Royal Princess,* the Royal Navy finally learns why their ships blow up and plan design changes for new warships, and prohibit the sloppy handling of explosives and propellants.

On November 7, 1916, the Presidential election competed President Taft and Vice President La Follette against the Democrat candidate William Jennings Bryan, who ran for the fourth time. The American public did not want any part of the European war. Taft campaigned on the theme *He kept us out of the war.* Vice President La Follette, an ardent voice of *America First*, toured across the country touting the value of peace.

Bryan campaigned against high tariffs and corruption in the Republican Party. The voters re-elected Taft and LaFollette with 55% of the vote.

The Mexican civil war continued, and the nation dissolved into fiefdoms controlled by various generals. The United States occupation of Chihuahua and Sonora became permanent. President Taft appointed General Pershing as the military governor of both previously Mexican states.

An additional 50,000 soldiers reinforced Pershing in preparation for military actions to end the bloodshed. A United States Navy task force led by the battleships USS Florida and USS Utah, plus the aircraft carrier USS Langley assembled at Galveston, TX. Five-thousand Marines gathered, waiting for transport ships.

On November 16, Emperor Franz Joseph I of Austria dies at the age of 86 from complications of pneumonia. Archduke Franz Ferdinand assumes the throne as Emperor Franz Ferdinand I. His coronation would wait for the mandatory 30-day period of mourning

With 1916 drawing to a close on the Western Front, battle lines are mostly in the same areas as the start of the year.

Casualties on both sides total in the millions, and the combatant's economies are on the brink of collapse. King Albert of Belgium sends a secret telegram to President Taft asking him to chair a peace conference in Washington DC. Coincidentally, Kaiser Wilhelm II also sent a note suggesting that President Taft organize a peace conference.

Encouraged, President Taft instructed Secretary of State Knox to send out peace feelers to the ambassadors of the United Kingdom, France, Italy, Austria-Hungary, Bulgaria, the Ottoman Empire, Japan, and Russia, to determine if an appetite for a peace conference existed.

Chapter 29

In January 1917, backdoor diplomacy between Secretary of State Knox and the combatant ambassadors in Washington DC seemed to have promise. Belgium favored negotiations. The French gave a non-committal answer. The German Ambassador Johann Heinrich von Bernstorff enthusiastically endorsed the proposal. The British Ambassador, Sir Cecil Spring-Rice, initially hesitant, provided approval when he realized his rival Johann Heinrich von Bernstorff would attend. The Russian Ambassador George Bakhmetev would not commit as Tsar Nicholas was incommunicado leading the Russian Army at the front.

The new Austria-Hungary Ambassador Count Adam Tarnowski arrived on January 27 as the personal representative of Emperor Franz Joseph I. He presented his credentials to President Taft, then requested a meeting with Taft and Knox. Taft granted the request, and he and Knox met Count Tarnowski the next day.

Following coffee and doughnuts, Count Tarnowski forwarded a dramatic proposal. First, Emperor Franz Joseph wanted to withdraw from the war status quo. He would agree to a cease-fire if the other combatants would also agree. When asked about the Empire's captured territory in Romania, Count Tarnowski indicated that everything was negotiable.

Secretary of State Knox then brought up Serbia, which was a delicate topic due to the assassination attempt on Franz Joseph, and the murder of his beloved wife, Sophie. Anticipating this topic, Count Tarnowski indicated that the Emperor would negotiate the possible restoration of Serbia's independence in return for a non-aggression pact.

Knox and Taft were impressed with Count Tarnowski's sincerity. Knox asked if Austria-Hungary would object to the Serbian Ambassador in exile attendance at the conference. Count Tarnowski accepted, indicating he welcomed the opportunity to end this infernal war before it destroys all of

Europe.

The Russian Revolution began with bread riots in Petrograd on February 23. Over 50,000 civilians mostly women marched, chanting slogans against the rationing, the war, and the monarchy. Union strikers quickly joined the women and riots broke out. Police fired into the crowd, which inflamed the situation.

Tsar Nicholas, involved with an offensive at Riga, accepted the Empress' assurances that the riots were overblown. Feeling assured, he ordered the continuation of the attacks. The next day, over 250,000 chanting demonstrators marched on the government institutions, breaking into buildings and starting fires.

On February 25, Tsar Nicholas ordered the military governor to quell the revolt. However, by then, the rebellion was out of control. Over 400,000 demonstrators demanding the end of the monarchy controlled the city. Statues of the Tsar were torn down across the city. Initially, the soldiers fired into the crowd, killing hundreds of demonstrators. Enraged, the demonstrators destroyed government buildings. Tens of thousands of demonstrators marched on the army headquarters. Women and Children led the demonstrators shouting will you kill your children, mothers, and grandmothers? Ordered to shoot the demonstrators, the troops mutinied, joined the demonstrators, and began to slaughter their officers.

On February 27, Tsar Nicholas returned to the Alexander Palace outside Petrograd, with his capital city entirely under control of the rioters and rebellious troops. The Duma established a Provisional Government and declared itself to be the governing body of the Russian Empire. Two days later Tsar Nicholas abdicated the throne for himself and the Crown Prince Alexi. Tsar Nicholas nominated his brother Grand Duke Michael Alexandrovich as his successor.

A Duma committee interviewed the presumed future Tsar to determine his political leanings. Grand Duke Michael's reputation assumed he would be a model Constitutional Monarch. Michael himself told the committee he would only accept the crown if the Duma elected him.

When the Duma met to vote, cognizant of the mood of the demonstrators and rebellious troops, it voted to end the monarchy and declare Russia to be a republic. The Provisional Government placed the Tsar's Royal Family, including Michael, his wife, and son under protective custody at the Alexander Palace.

With the Russian Army in turmoil, the German Army began an offensive, capturing Riga, the rest of the province of Latvia, and invaded the region of Estonia. With the fall of the Estonian provincial capital Reval, the German troops were only one-hundred miles from Petrograd. A series of blizzards prevented any other offensive actions. The German forces obtained supplies by sea. The High Seas Fleet escorted the convoys from Germany to Riga and Reval.

The Russian Ambassador to the United States, George Bakhmetev, appointed by the Tsar, did not have a new portfolio. The provisional government requested he attend the peace conference as an observer only until the replacement Ambassador arrived.

Pope Benedict XV requested to send a Papal Ambassador to the peace conference. He wanted to assist in ending what he termed *The suicide of civilized Europe.* President Taft welcomed the prospect of a papal envoy. The Pope appointed his Secretary of State Cardinal Eugenio Pacelli as Papal Nuncio to the conference, scheduled by President Taft for May 1 at Breton Woods, NH.

Trying to improve their negotiating position both the French and the British launched massive attacks. The British army fought the 3rd battle of Ypres, and the French began the Nivelle Offensive on German positions on the ridge north of the Aisne River. The allies attacked with 850,000 soldiers and 128 tanks. The German defenders numbered 480,000. In the early days of the battle, Brigadier General Robert Pomeroy led his brigade of 8,000 soldiers drawn from the original BEF. The British used Pomeroy's veterans as shock troops, working with tanks to establish a breakthrough. After initial success, which penetrated two miles, the German Army counterattacked, pushing the allies back to the original lines, and turned both offensives into catastrophic failures, with allied casualties over 450,000 soldiers and the destruction of eighty-five tanks. Pomeroy's brigade covered the retreat, losing over fifty-percent of its soldiers

Towards the end of the battle, the French Army mutinied, refused to advance, and 27,000 soldiers deserted. Morale plummeted. Before the attacks, the generals told the soldiers that the offensive would end the war. Fortunately for the French, the Germans did not know of the mutiny. A counter-offensive could have broken the spirit of the French Army.

Cautiously, Von Hindenberg weighed his options. The British and French armies suffered enormous losses. However, his army also suffered greatly. A counter-offensive could easily be unsuccessful, especially if the British and French brought in fresh re-enforcements. With peace negotiations set to begin, Von Hindenberg decided to strengthen his defenses. Except for sporadic artillery barrages, a lull in fighting descended onto the Western Front.

Chapter 30

Treaty of Washington

On April 30, the delegations from the warring nations including Austria-Hungary Belgium, Bulgaria, France, Germany, Great Britain, Italy, Japan, and the Ottoman Empire began to arrive. Representatives from the conquered nations of Serbia and Montenegro came as observers. The Russian Ambassador, without instructions from the Provisional Government, remained as an observer.

Secretary of State Knox and the Papal Nuncio, Cardinal Eugenio Pacelli, arrived a day early for a pre-conference meeting. As neutral parties, they agreed to move among the delegations to find points of agreement to bring to the table. In strict confidence, Knox outlined the Austro-Hungarian position.

King Albert I of Belgium arrived, met with Knox and Cardinal Pacelli. The King, a devout Catholic, ruled a country which suffered German occupation of ninety-percent of its territory. He outlined his peace proposal of *No victors, No Vanquished*. Albert considered that such a resolution of the war would be in the best interests of Belgium, and the future stability of Europe.

If the Germans evacuated Belgium, he would take Belgium out of the war. Knox and Cardinal Pacelli assured King Albert that other un-named delegations also shared his sentiments. The Cardinal asked the King to find a way to insert his proposal into his comments during the opening round-table. Albert readily agreed.

Knox introduced Cardinal Pacelli to the Austro-Hungarian Ambassador Count Tarnowski. Following the obligatory small talk, Knox excused himself to meet with other delegations. The Cardinal asked Count Tarnowski's position at the peace conference. Tarnowski detailed Emperor Franz Ferdinand's proposals, and under delicate questioning also revealed that Austria-Hungary would agree to vacate

Serbia and Montenegro with proper security considerations. The Cardinal, without disclosing any confidential information, assured Count Tarnowski that Austria-Hungary would observe delegations who thought much the same way.

Knox met separately with the German, British and French ambassadors to gauge their positions. The German Ambassador Johann Heinrich von Bernstorff was favorable for the development of a resolution. He reminded Knox that the Kaiser originally proposed a peace conference back in December.

The French Ambassador Jean Jules Jusserand demanded German withdrawal from all conquered territory and reparations, solely blaming Germany for the war. He also required the return of Alsace-Lorraine and control of the Saar coalfields.

Sir Cecil was more circumspect in his position. The British Empire casualties numbered over one-million-seven-hundred-thousand with over one-million-one hundred-thousand killed in action. During the war, the Empire soldiers occupied most of the former German colonies. Great Britain's involvement in the war began with the invasion of Belgium. Before then they worked to bring the war to a close with negotiations. Sir Cecil indicated the Crown was open to a negotiated settlement.

On May 1 at 9:00 am the conference convened. Secretary of State Knox gavelled the gathering to order. As host of the meeting, Knox Spoke first. He began:

"Gentlemen, except for Belgium, the Papal Nuncio, and the United Kingdom, all the warring nations at this table are mutually complicit in starting this war. The interlocking alliances brought Europe face to face with a mile-high pyramid style bonfire, which only needed a spark to ignite. That spark was the attempted assassination of the Arch Duke Franz Ferdinand, and the murder of his wife. While the Serbian government was not responsible for the actions of Serbian nationalists, individual Serbian intelligence officers knew of the plan but did not try to stop the plot.

The Austro-Hungarian government, anxious to punish Serbia made unreasonable demands, then declared war. The interlocking alliances required the other European powers to declare war on each other without first suffering offense." Nodding to Sir Cecil, Knox continued.

"Of the major powers, only Great Britain attempted to seek a negotiated settlement. However, when Germany invaded Belgium and refused to withdraw, Great Britain honored her mutual defense treaty with Belgium and declared war on Germany.

Since that time, the blood of over 12,000,000 soldiers, sacrificed on the altar of negligent diplomacy, demands an answer. None of you believed that the war would happen. When it did, all of you predicted it would be over by Christmas. However, you did not indicate what Christmas. The time has come to an end this madness. We are here together at this table to end it now."

As previously arranged, the individual countries had five minutes of opening comments. Count Tarnowski stood up to speak for Austria-Hungary. He began: Austria-Hungary bears a heavy burden of this war. The previous government moved too hastily to accuse Serbia, which now lies vanquished following a stout defense. Austria-Hungary paid with the lives of over 2,000,000 brave soldiers for this miscalculation. Serbia paid with its independence." Looking over at the Serbian representatives, Count Tarnowski continued.

"Emperor Franz Ferdinand has instructed me to seek a peaceful resolution to this war, and when accomplished, the Emperor empowered me to negotiate directly with the Serbian and Montenegrin representatives to resolve our conflict. If this damnable war has taught us anything, it is we must learn to live in peace." With that closing statement, he sat down to loud applause.

King Albert stood next. He began by stating: "I thank Count Tarnowski for his honesty and willingness to find a peaceful solution. Belgium is also willing to push for peace. My nation has been devastated, with over ninety-percent of our territory conquered and occupied by the German Army. This occupation and the destruction brought on by war destroyed the fabric of Belgium's society. However, if the German government orders its army to begin a total withdrawal forthwith, and guarantees our borders, Belgium will withdraw from the war." Following a stunned silence, the applause drowned out the French denunciations.

The Ambassador from Bulgaria Stephan Panaretov spoke next. Bulgaria entered the war in 1915 to recover provinces lost to Serbia in 1913 during the 2nd Balkan War. The Bulgarian Army also assisted in the defeat of Romania in 1916; recapturing the region of Dobruja. Panaretov indicated Bulgaria would also cease hostilities, and begin negotiations with its neighbors.

The French Ambassador Jean Jules Jusserand stood up to speak. He stared at King Albert, who stared back. Following an uncomfortable moment, Jusserand looked at Germany's Ambassador von Bernstorff who steepled his fingers as he stared back.

Jusserand then looked at Sir Cecil, who looked back with raised eyebrows. Knox spoke “Mr. Ambassador,” which brought Jusserand back to the moment. He realized that his bellicose comments from the day before would not work. The mood in the room was leaning to end the war. He trembled as he began.

“France is suffering the German occupation and devastation of the northern portion of our country. Almost two-million brave French soldiers died on those battlefields, and a million of our citizens are displaced. Certainly, we must bring this war to an end, but that end must be just. The blood of our fallen requires justice for their lives. France is willing to negotiate a peaceful end to this calamity.”

The German Ambassador Johann Heinrich von Bernstorff spoke next. He stated: “We could endlessly discuss who declared war on whom first, or who fired the first shot. We are not here to discuss that. We are here to end this war. I have been empowered by the Kaiser to offer a cease-fire to begin at midnight May 4, 1917. That will give all present time to notify their field commanders. I am here to declare that the German Army will not fire another shot unless attacked. Millions of brave soldiers on all sides are dead. No more should die while we talk. Germany will immediately begin negotiations to implement measures to end this war. In summary, the German Army will stand down, and we urge all other parties to do the same."

Reporters, seated in the gallery above the conference room bolted from the gathering to be the first to telephone the news of the German offer for an immediate cease-fire. The delegates were all on their feet, applauding. Knox banged the gavel to restore order. Slowly the noise abated. Knox banged the gavel again, then looked at Sir Cecil and said: "Mr. Ambassador the floor is yours."

Sir Cecil stood and stated: "When Germany stands down the soldiers and sailors of the British Empire and Commonwealth of Nations will also stand down. We can negotiate the details later. However, the fighting must stop now." With that, he strode over to von Bernstorff and offered his hand. Von Bernstorff shook it avidly then both raised the handclasp in the air. Camera light bulbs flashed, and an iconic picture of the former enemies raising clasped hands under the headline C E A S E F I R E becomes front-page news throughout the United States and Europe.

Bi-lateral negotiations consume the rest of the day. Von Bernstorff meets privately with King Albert to arrange for the withdrawal of all German troops, with the departure to begin as soon as the cease-fire is signed.

Knox acts as a mediator between Von Bernstorff and Jean Jules Jusserand. Too much hatred, too many deaths, and too much destruction of French territory in Germany's occupation of Northern France allow Jusserand to participate in a face to face meeting. Jusserand demands reparations as just compensation. Von Bernstorff replies that Germany too suffered millions of casualties, but are willing to honor the cease-fire and evacuate mineral-rich portions of France.

Knox finally says to Jusserand: "Jules, the mood of the conference, and the jubilation spreading around the world is evidence that the world wants this agreement. Do you want to be the single Ambassador who thwarted their desires? The names of the signers of the agreement will soon be forgotten. However, history will forever remember the name of the one who stood in the way of peace." Jusserand started to object, hesitated for several moments, then with a heavy sigh h,e agreed to the cease-fire and to sign the subsequent Armistice Agreement.

Chapter 31

On May 4, at the joint invitation of the Speaker of the House of Representatives, and the President of the Senate, President Taft and Secretary of State Knox hosted the signing of the Armistice by all the delegates in the Rotunda of the Capitol Building in Washington DC. Celebrations began with fireworks displays. Others quietly filled churches in celebratory prayer services. Amid all the excitement, nobody notices the early departure of the Italian and Japanese delegations.

Following the acquisitions of the German naval Base at Tsisingo, China, and the Marshall and Caroline Islands, Japan quietly incorporated the newly acquired territories into their overseas empire; and had no intention of returning them to Germany. With their growing Imperial Navy, now the fourth largest in the world, the Japanese felt secure in their position.

The Italians, following the signing ceremony, departed the conference very disgruntled. In 1915, the Allies promised them territory in Austria, and along the Dalmatian Coast. During the war, the Italian Army sustained over 700,000 casualties – all for nothing! Italy was not strong enough to stand alone. The hope existed that bi-lateral negotiations with Austria-Hungary would prove fruitful.

The Russian Provisional Government divided by disputes between the Mensheviks and the Bolsheviks never sent an ambassador to the peace conference. Therefore, none of the conference provisions applied to Russia.

The Austro-Hungarians, exhausted by war, requested the Papal Nuncio visit Petrograd and offer to extend the cease-fire. However, without a commitment to peace, the Russian border remained fortified.

The German Government also was

interested in a cease-fire with Russia but decided not to surrender its Russian conquests. The Russian Revolution brought instability to the area. The new Russian government, currently dominated by socialists, had the Royal Family under house arrest. The German Government's primary concern was to prevent that revolution from spreading into Germany. Therefore, the German Army erected fortifications all along the new borders.

May 5th dawned on the Western Front. For the first time since the start of the war, quiet reigns. Some soldier begins to sing. The song is picked up on both sides, and soon singing replaces the sound of gunfire.

Then a strange sight appears. A wounded cavalry horse stumbles across no-mans-land, trips over a roll of barbed wire, falls, rises painfully and rears up trying to free itself. Then one English soldier stands up, spreads his open hands wide and slowly approaches the horse, trying to untangle the legs. The tightly wrapped wire cuts into the horse's legs.

The English soldier feels a tap on his shoulders; a German soldier hands over his wire cutters. Together they free the horse, which rises and trots away. The English soldier points to himself and says, Bill. The German soldier gestures to himself and saying, Willie. Both men laugh and embrace. In minutes, no-mans-land is full of soldiers from both sides, celebrating, sharing cigarettes, laughing together. The War is over.

In Belgium, the German Army marches east, back into Germany. Cautiously, several miles behind, with King Albert riding a white horse leading the way, the Belgian Army advances through villages, small towns and finally into Brussels. The populous is jubilant and cheering crowds welcome the Belgian soldiers home.

In Paris, the French Army marches in columns through the Arch of Triumph. Cheering crowds are celebrating. French territory is free of German soldiers for the first time in almost three years.

In London, Brigadier General Robert Pomeroy, in dress uniform leads three-thousand survivors from the original BEF past flag-waving crowds into Westminster Square, and up to a reviewing stand. General Pomeroy locates his wife and two children on the reviewing platform as he is brought up the stairs. The family shares a warm embrace to the calls "Kiss her" from the soldiers. Pomeroy then walks to the front of the platform and is greeted by General Douglas Haig who awards him the Victoria Cross for his rearguard decisions at the 3rd Battle of Ypres.

During his prepared remarks, Pomeroy praises the BEF, for its bravery, initiative, and sacrifice. At the end of his comments, he steps away from the podium and salutes his troops. As one, they snap to attention and return the salute. Then the cheers begin.

Royal Guards escort General Pomeroy and his family into a waiting limousine for the short trip to Buckingham Palace. There, in an age-old ceremony, Pomeroy kneels before King George V on a Knighting Pillow.

King George V, using a ceremonial sword, taps the flat side first on the right shoulder, then on the left shoulder. Pomeroy then stands up and accepts the insignia of The Order of the British Empire from King George V.

Following a reception, the Pomeroys depart Buckingham Palace. The Pomeroy family's chauffeured limousine drives them back to Pomeroy Manor. Two weeks later, a new oil painting, of General Pomeroy in his dress uniform wearing his Victoria Cross and the Order of the British Empire insignia adorns the gallery.

President Taft's prestige as a world leader and peacemaker make him the odds-on-favorite for the Nobel Peace Prize. Of all the world powers, only the United States escaped unscarred by the conflict. Over twelve million soldiers died in battle, and a like number of civilians perished as collateral damage from the warfare and starvation. Belgian civilians suffered excessively.

President Taft's policy of America First did

not preclude humanitarian aid to the suffering European populations. Taft appointed a successful industrialist Herbert Hoover to lead American Food Aid to Europe. For two and one-half years, Hoover based himself in London. The American Relief Association distributed over two-million tons of food to Europe. This food aid saved an estimated 10,500,000 civilians from starvation. The Belgian city of Leuven named a central square Hooverplein in honor of him.

While the European powers decimated their civilians and military's in unending conflict, the United States grew stronger. With the addition of the six South Dakota Class super Dreadnoughts, the United States Navy equaled the Royal Navy in size and surpassed it in quality, protection, and armaments.

Chapter 32

The Peace Dividend

America First, the official policy of the Taft Administration based itself on the doctrine of peace through strength. The six South Dakota Class battleship's radical redesign trunked the two funnels into one structure, which allowed four sixteen-inch gun turrets, with a total of twelve sixteen-inch guns. These gun turrets elevated to 46 degrees had a range of 26 miles. The battleships had a secondary battery of sixteen six-inch guns. Increased watertight compartments protected against torpedos, and improved survivability. The warships speed increased to twenty-eight knots with the new electric turbine engines.

These improvements, combined with the four Colorado Class Battleships, equipped with nine, sixteen-inch guns, created the most powerful fleet of warships in the world. The United States Navy could project unsurpassed sea power. The Panama Canal provided easy access to the Atlantic and Pacific fleets.

The USN previously experimented with aircraft carriers. The Navy converted the collier USS Jupiter to a warship, by removing the superstructure and installing a flight deck.

USS Langley

Measuring 542 feet long and renamed USS Langley the aircraft carrier had one aircraft elevator leading to an open hangar deck, with a capacity of thirty-six aircraft. Armament consisted of four, five-inch single guns, located on the hanger deck two forward, two aft.

Experiments with flight operations led to the decision to convert two Lexington Class battlecruiser hulls to aircraft carriers. The United States Navy rejected the completion of the battlecruisers, as the battles of Dogger Bank and Jutland demonstrated their lack of survivability in combat with other Dreadnoughts. 1922 became the estimated target date for the completion of the aircraft carriers USS Lexington and USS Saratoga. Both carrier's gunnery included four, superfiring twin-gun turrets of eight-inch guns fore and aft of the control tower.

USS Lexington

The aircraft carriers were 887 feet in length, and 107 feet at the beam. The size allowed them to pass through the Panama Canal. The new electric turbine engines allowed these warships to have a speed of thirty-three knots.

$25,000,000 in funds for the conversion came from the sale of two Mississippi Class pre-Dreadnoughts: *USS Idaho* and *USS Mississippi* in 1914, and two Connecticut Class pre-dreadnought battleships, *USS Minnesota* and *USS New Hampshire* in 1916 to Greece. These warships, obsolete in the United States Navy became prize warships in the Greek Navy, which sent crews to steam them from Norfolk, Virginia to Greece. The Greek Navy renamed them *Lemnos, Kilkis, Troas,* and *Smyrna*.

The doctrine of peace through strength was an expensive proposition. The United States Navy decided to eliminate the older obsolete pre-Dreadnoughts, and also the obsolescent original design Dreadnoughts. Liberia, flush with diamonds purchased the Dreadnoughts *USS South Carolina* and *USS Michigan* for a total of $20,000,000. Liberian officers and crew took possession at Norfolk, Virginia. Following a two-week shakedown cruise off the Chesapeake Bay, the Liberians steamed for Monrovia.

The Baltic Sea and the North Sea were perfect locations for the remaining Connecticut Class Battleships. The Nordic Union desired to have self-defense forces. Denmark Purchased the *USS Connecticut.* Sweden-Norway purchased *USS Vermont, USS Kansas,* and *USS Louisiana* for $6,000,000 each. Danish and Swedish crews took possession at Norfolk and steamed home.

The United States Navy divested the country of six battleships they no longer needed. The warship sale returned $49,000,000 to the United States Treasury, which earmarked the money for future naval expansion. The navy de-commissioned the earlier pre-Dreadnoughts and used them as target ships or sold them for scrap.

Mexico City

The Constitutionalist Party won control of Mexico during the June elections in1917. They passed laws expropriating businesses and resources owned by the United States and foreign interests. The United States continued the occupation of Chihuahua and Sonora resulted in anti-American riots in Vera Cruz and Mexico City. The rioters burned American owned or affiliated businesses and murdered over 50 United States citizens. Hundreds of United States citizens went into hiding or sought refuge in the United States Embassy in Mexico City or in other Consulates.

General Pershing moved south with fifty-thousand troops towards Mexico City. The United States Navy task force led by the battleships USS Florida, USS Utah, and the aircraft carrier USS Langley landed five-thousand Marines at Vera Cruz. Advancing quickly to the besieged United States Consulate, the Marines suppressed the riots. Aircraft from the USS Langley scouted for concentrations of rioters or Mexican forces. Following brief resistance, the Mexican police and army soldiers threw down their weapons and surrendered.

The warlord armies facing General Pershing's forces melted away. Within one week, Pershing's army entered Mexico City and broke the siege at the United States Embassy. During a week-long street to street battle, Pershing's soldiers killed or captured the rioters, police and Mexican soldiers. Large sections of Mexico City burned during the fighting.

The Constitutionalist President of Mexico, Venustiano Carranza and three-thousand soldiers retired to the fortress of Chapultepec. Pershing surrounded the fort laying siege and beginning negotiations.

Chapultepec would be a hard nut to crack, particularly with modern weapons and machine guns. Trench warfare in Europe grimly proved the cost of a frontal attack on an entrenched foe. Modern artillery could reduce Chapultepec to ruins. However, those ruins would also provide the Mexican defender's more ideal defensive positions.

With the leadership of the Mexican National Army under siege in Mexico City, Emiliano Zapata rampaged through southern Mexico. Zapata and General Pancho Villa united in opposing Carranza. Their army advanced east to conquer the Yucatan Peninsula and south to the Honduras border.

Ten-Thousand United States Army reinforcements landed at Vera Cruz, and with the Marines advanced towards Mexico City. With aircraft sweeping ahead, the army and cavalry regiments overwhelmed pockets of resistance from the Mexican National Army.

Following a siege of 30-days, President Carranza realized there was no chance that he could reassert control after the United States military left. The army of Zapata and General Villa controlled all of Mexico south of Mexico City. Zapata and Villa signed a peace accord with General Pershing recognizing Zapata's control of the territory he occupied. The United States Army was firmly in control of the rest of Mexico. Carranza negotiated safe-passage for himself, his family, and top government officials to Vera Cruz. There they would board a Spanish vessel for exile in Spain.

October 1, 1917

Following the departure of Carranza and his followers, Pershing sat down with Zapata and Villa to negotiate peace. Pershing's terms were harsh.

1. The United States would annex the Mexican states of Senora, Chihuahua, Coahuila, Nuevo Leon, and Tamaulipas. These states bordered the American states of

Texas, New Mexico, and Arizona. Over one-hundred United States citizens died in border incursions by Mexican military forces.

2. Mexico would receive Fifty-million gold dollars in compensation.

3. American corporations would be allowed to resume their business interests in Mexico. However, they would be subject to Mexican taxation and would be subject to Mexican laws.

4. Full diplomatic relations would resume.

5. Mexico would accept protection from the United States.

Zapata and Villa protested the harshness of the terms. General Pershing reminded Zapata that he considered himself the President of the ordinary people. If Zapata refused to sign the peace treaty, Pershing with his available military forces would attack all of Mexico. The United States Navy would close down all Mexican seaports. Mexico's economy would never recover, and ordinary people would starve.

Reluctantly, Zapata and Villa signed the treaty, which would require ratification by the Mexican Congress and the United States Senate. With the acceptance by both parties, the United States Army would retire behind the new borders.

Chapter 33

Vienna, Austria

The Austrian Prime Minister Count Heinrich von Clam-Martinic and his Hungarian counterpart Istvan Tesla greeted the Serbian Prime Minister Nikola Pasic at von Clam-Martinic's office in the Austrian Parliament Building. The war was over, and it was time to return sovereignty to Serbia. The withdrawal of the Austro-Hungarian Army from Serbia proceeded at a steady pace. The Bulgarian Army already evacuated from most of Macedonia, excepting provinces previously held by Bulgaria before the 2nd Balkan war.

The three Prime Ministers gathered to develop a non-aggression and security pact. With full diplomatic relations restored, unresolved disagreements would go to mandatory arbitration. A strong feeling of distrust still existed. However, the terrible price of over 500,000 deaths in the war demanded the restoration of a semblance of trust. The first step, an intelligence liaison office, based at each nation's embassy, would meet monthly to share intelligence on tips about known or suspected subversive activities against each country. Critical information was to be passed on as soon as it developed. The three Prime Ministers agreed that given the circumstances this was a good beginning.

Following the departure of the Serbian Prime Minister, Count Heinrich von Clam-Martinic and Istvan Tesla accepted a carriage ride to Schonbrunn Palace for a scheduled meeting with Emperor Franz Joseph.

The Emperor, satisfied with the progress of talks with Serbia, moved on to a controversial topic. Specifically, the further division of the administration of the empire. He points to a map on the wall showing the nationalities comprising the Austro-Hungarian Empire. They all acknowledged the tensions war brought to the realm, and the divisions threatening to pull it apart.

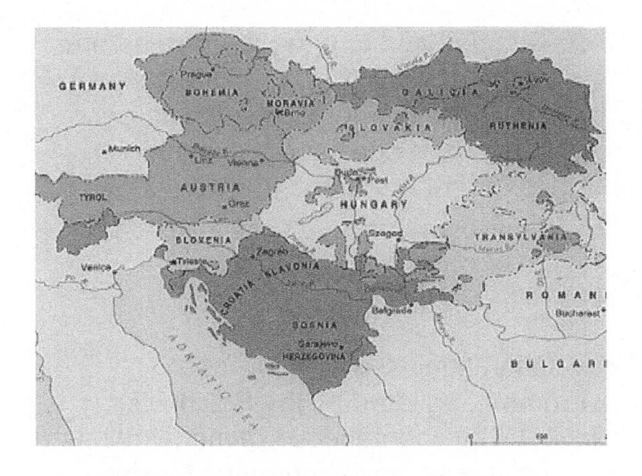

The Emperor proposed nine separate kingdoms within the empire, all to be united by a common constitution. The two principal domains Austria and Hungary would each have co-equal prime ministers, and alternating national parliamentary sessions. The other kingdoms would have deputy prime ministers. Each would elect its assembly called a Diet, which would send representatives to the national Parliaments meeting of Buda Pest and Vienna.

The Emperor empowered the two Prime Ministers to assemble a convention to draft the constitution and to bring it to him before years end. The Emperor would be the king of the individual kingdoms. However, each entity would have considerable latitude in self-government within the framework of the constitution.

Petrograd, July 3.

A revolution against the Provisional Government, agitated by the Bolsheviks, broke out with spontaneous demonstrations by the Petrograd Soviet, the First Machine Gun Regiment and the Kronstadt sailors who murdered their officers and an admiral. Prime Minister Alexander Kerensky and Defense Minister Prince Lvov commanded troops which violently suppressed the rioters.

Lenin fled to Finland. However, the secret police arrested Trotsky and Stalin as they boarded a boat to follow Lenin. Private trials for both agitators led to summary execution. Guards shot both men in the back of the head, and subsequently in the legs, and shoulders. The official line indicated the prisoners died attempting to escape.

The Bolshevik Soviet in Moscow raised the Red Banner of revolt. Civil war engulfed Russia with each side, fielding thousands of loyal soldiers. Lenin returned assuming command of the Bolsheviks. In November, at the Battle of Kursk, Prince Lvov's Provisional Army decisively defeated the Bolsheviks, who retreated across the Ural Mountains. The Russian winter set in, eliminating further combat.

Simultaneously, independence movements broke out in Ukraine, and the Caucasus Mountains provinces of Armenia, Azerbaijan, and Georgia. The Caucasus provinces, united in common cause and defeated the Russian Army dispatched to bring them to heel. In Ukraine, the Russian Army suffered defeat 50-miles from Kiev.

In March and April 1918, Lenin's Bolsheviks reinforced by Siberians launched a counter-offensive, capturing Moscow and threatening Petrograd. Fearing a Bolshevik victory in Russia, Germany intervened. General Ludendorff assembled an army of

100,000 German soldiers in Estonia. Ludendorff spread the rumor that he assigned a brigade of five-thousand German Cavalry to rescue the Tsar's family from capture by the Bolsheviks. Lenin took the bait and rushed towards Petrograd to intercept the Germans and capture the Tsar.

Between Pskov and Gatchina Lenin's army encountered a firmly entrenched German blocking force. Sensing a trap, Lenin retreated towards Pskov. There he met 50,000 German soldiers blocking his retreat. Blocked by the German army to his north and south, Lenin ordered a desperate attack to the north, attempting to break through to Petrograd.

German machine guns cut through the attacking Bolsheviks like a sickle through wheat. Lenin's army, trapped between the advancing German hammer from their rear could not break through the anvil to their front. The advancing Germans virtually annihilated the trapped Red Army. Lenin ordered the remnants to retreat through the swamps. Fresh snow on the ground revealed escape routes. Pursuing German cavalry ran them down, killing most and capturing Lenin and his surviving senior staff.

Diplomatic messages sent to Kerensky arranged for the turnover of Lenin to Prince Lvov, in return for the release into permanent exile of the Royal Family. General Ludendorff met with Prince Lvov at the Alexander Palace to make the exchange. General Ludendorff then marched his army back into Estonia.

Prince Lvov empaneled a court-martial, as Lenin commanded the Bolshevik forces. The court-martial convicted Lenin and his senior staff of treason and sentenced them to death. The next morning the condemned men were publicly executed by firing squad. The Russians widely published newsreels of the execution to prove that Lenin was dead. Without their leaders, the Bolshevik movement crumbled.

In June, negotiations between Russian and Ukranian leaders resulted in a peaceful resolution. Ukraine, in return for self-government in an autonomous republic, joined a Federation of Russian Republics, with Russia, Belarus, Kazakhstan, and the Far Eastern Republic led by General Alexander Kolchak, a former Tsarist general.

The Far Eastern Republic also was an autonomous, self-governing state compromising the Maritime Provinces at Vladivostok, and westward along the Manchurian and Mongolian borders. The Russian civil war ended with Tsarist Russia transformed into a democratically elected federation of republics.

The Russian Royal Family, descendants of Queen Victoria, accepted exile in Great Britain. There they resided in a wing at Balmoral Castle in Scotland. On November 15, during the worldwide flu epidemic, both Tsar Nicholas and Prince Alexi died within hours of each other. The world leaders all attended the state funerals, including Alexander Kerensky.

With both the former Tsar and Tsarevich dead; Prime Minister Kerensky lifted the permanent exile. The former Empress, Alexandra Feodorovna, thanked Kerensky for his gesture but decided to remain at Balmoral with her daughters. Grand Duke Michael Alexandrovich renounced all ambitions for the Russian throne and renounced his titles. The renunciations enabled him, and his family to return to Russia with Kerensky.

Chapter 34

Fall of the Ottoman Empire

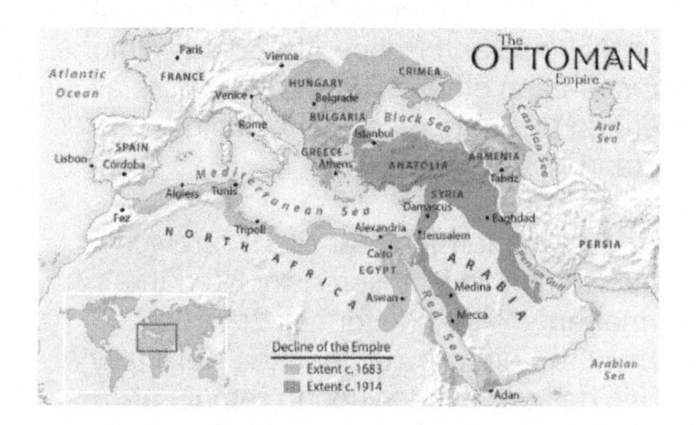

In 1683, the Ottoman Empire was the dominant power in Europe and the Middle East. By 1914, it shrank to a middle-eastern empire consisting of Thrace, Anatolia, Mesopotamia, Palestine, the Hejaz on the east coast of Arabian Peninsula including Mecca and Medina, and the west coast of the Arabian Peninsula bordering the Persian Gulf. The Sultan was also the Caliph and titular head of Islam.

In 1909, the Committee of Union and

Progress (CUP) won control of the government during the Young Turk Revolt. Declaring a constitutional monarchy, the CUP severely limited the powers of Sultan Mehmed V. The Sultan ordered them arrested. However, the Ottoman Army, very favorable to the Young Turks refused. The CUP then restricted the Sultan to ceremonial duties in Constantinople.

In 1915, the Sharif of Mecca, Hussein bin Ali declared an Arab revolt in Hejaz and announced the Hashemite Kingdom which extended into Palestine. He then n proclaimed himself to be Caliph, as the Sultan could not fulfill those duties. The Ottoman garrison, defeated in battle outside Mecca, retreated and entrenched in Medina where the Arabs established a siege.

Hussein's son Faisal, Sharif of Bagdad also rebelled and declared himself the King of Mesopotamia. The British assisted Faisal by landing troops at Basra drawing off Ottoman soldiers. The Arab Army besieged the Ottomans in Bagdad. The Bagdad Ottomans, mostly ethnic Arabs mutinied, forcing their commanders to surrender.

Faisal then enlisted the Arab Ottomans to force the British out of Basra.

The Kurds utilized the opportunity. Kurdish rebels defeated the Ottoman garrisons and declared the independent nation of Kurdistan. King Faisal led his Arab Army against the Kurds. However, the Kurdish Army decisively defeated Faisal's army at the battles of Kirkuk and Mosul.

Realizing he could not defeat the Kurds, Faisal recognized their independence. He then proposed an alliance against their common enemies, the Turks, and Persians. Quoting a middle-eastern proverb: "My enemies enemy is my friend," the Kurdish leader Simko Shikak allied Kurdistan with King Faisal and Mesopotamia.

The Ottoman Empire, reduced to Thrace, Anatolia, Syria, and Palestine launched an offensive against the Suez Canal. Logistically an attack on Suez is a difficult task as there are not any railroads across the Sinai. British aerial observation detected the Ottoman Army's approach. Thirty-thousand Indian and An-zak troops repulse the Ottoman attacks, forcing them to retreat into Palestine. The Ottomans beat back British counter-attacks at Gaza. The Ottoman attack produces a significant benefit. The British were required to leave substantial forces to defend the canal, minimizing support for their offensive activities in Gallipoli.

The Armistice signed in Washington DC on May 4. 1917 ended hostilities between the Allies and the Central Powers. However, local hostilities continued. The Ottoman Army commanded by Kemal Ataturk attempt to reclaim Kurdistan and Mesopotamia. Ataturk's forces are victorious in Western Syria, but the Kurds and Arabs repulsed them at Mosul.

On July 3, 1918, Sultan Mehmed V died without a male heir. His replacement was a cousin of Mehmed VI who was his closest male relative. In January 1919 Sultan Mehmed VI tried to reimpose imperial rule. The CUP opposed the Sultan as they wanted to maintain a constitutional monarchy. The former Defense Minister Enver Pasha led CUP forces.

The Nationalists commanded by Kemal Ataturk, wanted to abolish the monarchy. During the Young Turk revolt in 1908, Enver Pasha and Kemal Atturturk were friends. At the beginning of The Great War, they fought alongside each other in military activities against the Russians, British, and French.

However, political differences resulted in them being on opposite sides when the Turkish Civil War erupted. Enver Pasha led the CUP forces against Kemal Attaturk's Nationalists. The CUP and Nationalist armies fought in several inconclusive battles, bleeding the Ottoman Armies.

In July, the Greeks and the Bulgarians took advantage of the turmoil and invaded Thrace. The Bulgarians captured the provincial capital of Adrianople. They then advanced to the Black Sea, then down the coast towards Constantinople.

The Greek army of 100,000 soldiers, led by their General Victor Angelakas advanced to the Bosporus and with the Bulgarians and laid siege to Constantinople. A second

Greek army moved south and in October captured the Dardanelles Peninsula including Gallipoli.

With the Gallipoli forts silenced, the Greek Navy minesweepers cleared the mines in the Dardanelle channels, which allowed the pre-Dreadnought battleships *Lemnos, Kilkis, Troas,* and *Smyrna* plus the ironclad battleships *Psara, Hydra* and *Spetsai* to steam up the Dardanelles, bombarding the Turkish forts located in Anatolia into submission.

With the forts silenced, Greek troops landed taking possession of the fortified positions, and the Anatolia coastal areas. The Greek Navy then steamed into the Sea of Marmara. Troop transports accompanied, and following the intensive, bombardment by the battleships landed 50,000 soldiers on the east side of the Bosporus.

The CUP defenders of Constantinople appealed to Enver Pasha for assistance. However, he was unable to move his army due to negotiations with King Faisal and the Kurds to jointly defeat the Nationalist Army.

In return, he would recognize the independence of Mesopotamia and Kurdistan. However, he did order the Ottoman Navy to attempt to break the siege by attacking the Bulgarian Navy blockading Constantinople from the Black Sea.

On December 1, the Ottoman Navy steamed out of Trebizond. The capital warships included the pre-Dreadnought battleship *TCG Turgut Reis,* protected cruisers *TCG Hamidive* and *TCG Mecidive.* Smaller ships included the Torpedo cruisers TCG *Berk-i Satvet* and TCG *Peyk-i Sevket*, destroyers *TCG Samsun*, *TCG Basra* and *TCG Taşoz*, and torpedo boats *TCG Burak Reis*, *TCG Kemal Reis*, *TCG Îsâ Reis,* and TCG *Sakız*,

The mission involved destroying the Bulgarian Navy, and the relieve of the Black Sea blockade. After resupplying Constantinople, the fleet would steam into the Sea of Marmara to confront the Greek Navy. Accompanying the fleet were four freighters loaded with ammunition and supplies for the defenders.

The Bulgarian fleet consisted of one minesweeper, three torpedo boats, and ten gunboats. These warships were no match for the high caliber gunfire from *TCG Turgut Reis, TCG Hamidive,* and *TCG Mecidive* which sank four of the Bulgarian gunboats. The others retreated but were run down by the Ottoman torpedo cruisers and torpedo boats. Within two hours, all the Bulgarian warships littered the bottom of the Black Sea. The freighters docked and unloaded the needed supplies. The Ottoman Navy proceeded through the Bosporus to confront the Greek fleet.

The Ottoman fleet's single file battle line proceeded from the Bosporus to the Sea of Marmara, where the Greek fleet crossed their T. The Greek pre-dreadnought battleships *Lemnos, Kilkis, Troas,* and *Smyrna* steamed on a straight course firing broadsides into the Ottoman ships. The Ironclad battleships *Psara, Hydra,* and *Spetsai* added their weight of fire to the battle. Within thirty-minutes, *TCG Turgut Reis, TCG Hamidive,* and *TCG Mecidive* sustained four high caliber hits each, suffering substantial damage before being able to steam a parallel course to bring all their guns to bear. The uneven gun battle continued with the Ottoman warships out-gunned two to one.

The torpedo boats *TCG Burak Reis*, *TCG Kemal Reis*, *TCG Îsâ Reis,* and TCG *Sakız*, charged the Greek battleships firing torpedoes. Multiple hits from the Greek warships sank *TCG Kemal Reis*, *TCG Îsâ Reis*, and TCG *Sakız*. Two weapons struck the *Troas* resulting in a ten-degree list, which reduced her speed to twelve-knots. The *Psara, Hydra,* and *Spetsai* fired at the remaining Ottoman torpedo boat, driving it away from the stricken *Troas.*

The torpedo cruisers TCG *Berk-i Satvet* and TCG *Peyk-i Sevket* entered the battle shooting torpedoes from three tubes and firing their four-inch guns. *Psara* and *Hydra,* each struck by two of the weapons fell out of the battle line. TCG *Berk-i Satvet* hit multiple time by high-caliber shells exploded. TCG *Peyk-i Sevket* and *TCG Burak Reis* attacked *Psara* and *Hydra,* striking them with one torpedo each.

Unable to contain the flooding from three torpedo hits both warships rolled over and sank.

The gun battle between the Greek and Turkish battleships continued. The Greek battleships closed the distance to less than one mile. At the point-blank range, they could not miss, and high-caliber hits struck the Turkish warships turning them into burning wrecks. *Kilkis, Troas,* and *Smyrna* finished them off with torpedoes.

Observing the destruction of the other Ottoman warships, TCG *Peyk-i Sevket* and *TCG Burak Reis* fired torpedoes in the at the Greek battleships and escaped into the Bosporus as the battleships maneuvered to avoid the weapons.

With the Greek and Bulgarian Armies in control of Thrace, The Greek Army controlling the Dardanelles, and the land access from Anatolia, the capture of Constantinople became inevitable. Sultan Mehmed VI and his household boarded the royal yacht and escorted by TCG *Peyk-i Sevket* and *TCG Burak Reis* evacuated to his summer palace in Trebizond.

After the destruction of the Ottoman Navy, the Greek Navy swept through the Aegean capturing most of the Ottoman-held islands including Crete. On January 15, 1920, Constantinople fell from combined assaults from the land, and naval bombardment from the Sea of Marmara. For the first time since 1453, Christian religious services took place in Santa Sophia. The Greek and Bulgarian armies controlled the access to the Black Sea. The fall of the Ottoman Empire became a reality.

Chapter 35

Kemal Ataturk faced the problem of the CUP armies to the north and the alliance of the Kurds and Mesopotamians from the east. Ataturk attacked King Faisal's army, calculating it was the weakest. Ataturk's offensive drove the Mesopotamians back towards Bagdad. The Kurds attacked Ataturk's flank, allowing a Mesopotamian counter-attack to relieve the pressure on Bagdad.

Sealing Ataturk's fate, Caliph Hussein bin Ali declared Holy War against Kemal Ataturk and any who fought for him. The Hashemite Army of Hejaz marched through Palestine and attacked Syria from the south.

On March 25, the final battle occurred outside Damascus. Realizing that the allied armies outnumbered Ataturk's army by four to one, almost one-half of Ataturk's army deserted him, and melted away. Surrounded, the Nationalists attempted a breakout attacking to the north. Enver Pasha's CUP army, held, then counterattacked. Ataturk's loyal Nationalist divisions fought to the end. The Mesopotamian camel-mounted cavalry overran the final positions, capturing Kemal Ataturk. Together with Enver Pasha, Hussein bin Ali ordered the severely wounded, Ataturk to kneel, then beheaded him with a single sword cut.

Hussein bin Ali carved out the province of Syria as a kingdom for his eldest son and heir Abdullah. His realm extended from Mesopotamia to the Mediterranean Sea. With religious zeal, Abdullah began persecutions and forced conversions of the substantial Christian and Jewish populations in Syria. The Ottomans traditionally tolerated Christians and Jews as long as they paid the temple tax. Many Christians and Jews rose to high positions in the Ottoman government. The CUP also contained many Christian and Jewish members.

Great Britain, Italy, and France intervened, landing troops in Beruit, pushing Abdullah's forces out of the province of Lebanon and northwestern Palestine. Negotiations with

Abdullah established a French protectorate over an independent Lebanon. French troops remained as a garrison to protect Lebanon's majority Christian and substantial Jewish populations.

The Greco-Bulgarian alliance did not survive the fall of Constantinople. Arguments over who controlled which religious sites soon resulted in conflict. In a lightning 30-day war, the Greek army isolated the Bulgarian Army in Thrace, forcing its surrender. The Greek Navy bombarded the Bulgarian seaports along the Aegean Sea supporting a landing by Greek troops. Other Greek naval units established a blockade of the Bulgarian Black Sea ports. Bulgaria sued for peace ceding eastern and western Thrace to Greece.

Enver Pasha attacked the Greek conquests in western Anatolia. The Ottoman armies suffered defeats in their attempts to recapture Constantinople and Smyrna. They were more successful in the southwestern province of Antalya driving the Greeks back towards the sea until Greek trenches, mountain fortifications, and naval bombardment stopped the Ottoman advance. Both sides, exhausted by the war, agreed to a peace treaty sponsored by Germany and Austria-Hungary. Greece gave up their territory in Antalya province, in return for the Dedodanese Islands including Rhodes. Both sides agreed to a transfer of national minorities.

In August, the Sultan, angered by the loss of his empire, attempted to re-assert his authority over the government. The CUP, dissatisfied with the constant interference by the Sultan deposed him, declaring the Republic of Turkey. In Elections held in November, Enver Pasha became Turkeys first President. The deposed Sultan Mehmed VI accepted exile in Malta, then moved to the Italian Riviera.

Chapter 36

November 1920

The Presidential Election in the United States began a contentious political year. The early Republican front-runner Robert LaFollette angered the party leadership with his continued swing to the extreme Progressive wing of the party. Looking for a middle of the road candidate, the Republicans nominated the Massachusetts Governor Calvin Coolidge. For Vice President, they nominated Herbert Hoover, who led the American Relief Association to Europe immediately following The Great War.

The Democrats nominated James Cox the Governor of Ohio, and Franklin Delano Roosevelt from New York. The campaign became a referendum on the Taft Presidency.

The Irish Democrats deserted their party, as

Taft kept the United States out of the war. Great Britain decisively defeated the Irish Rebellions in 1916 and 19. About one-half of Irish Democrats voted Republican; the others refused to vote and stayed home. In Irish eyes, staying out of the war forced Great Britain to the bargaining table.

The mid-west German-Americans felt the same way. They overwhelmingly voted Republican.

The League of Nations, formed in Europe with headquarters in Geneva, also became an issue. Article 10 which committed signatory nations to wage any war declared by the League, was a non-starter. The Republican Party rejected the League. America First was the dominant theme throughout the country. Coolidge's affirmation of the Taft Doctrine – Peace Through Strength – resonated throughout the electorate.

The Democrats, while not supporting the League, rejected America First. They argued that the Taft Doctrine would force an international arms race. That arms race would destabilize the world, and bankrupt the nation.

On November 2, The Coolidge – Hoover ticket won with 61 percent of the popular vote, The Electoral College voted for Coolidge - Hoover by 454 to 127. The 1920 election became a benchmark, as with the ratification of the Nineteenth Amendment on August 18, 1920 women were allowed to vote. Their participation doubled the electorate and changed the electorate's face. Politicians now needed to pay attention to issues of primary interest to women.

Chapter 37

January 1921

Following over six years of almost constant warfare, the map of Europe and the middle east radically changed.

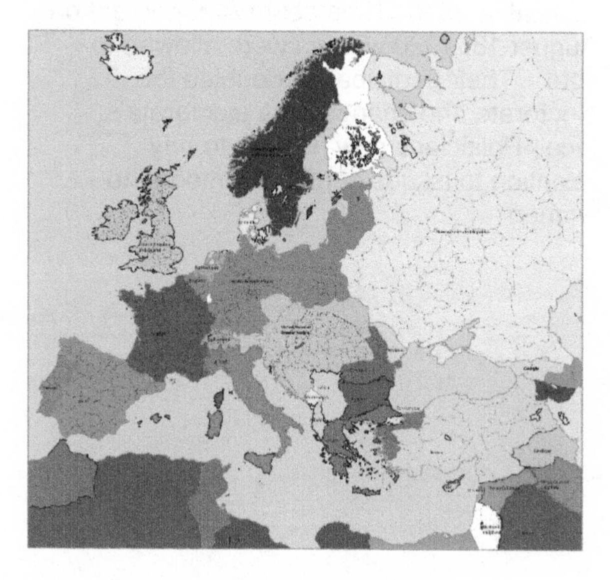

As a result of the Nordic Union, Sweden and Norway merged for the second time into a dual kingdom with duel capital cities of Stockholm and Oslo. Following the example of Austria-Hungary, each nation would have a Prime Minister, and the Parliament would meet in each capital in alternate years. Both countries had equal membership in Parliament. Both royal families would share the crown. The current Swedish King Gustav V named the former King of Norway Haakon VII as his heir.

The German Empire expanded east into the former Russian provinces of Poland, Estonia, Lithuania, and Latvia. Germany became the dominant power in Europe. The Kaiser's appointed princelings ruled in the semi-autonomous principalities of Poland, Estonia, Lithuania, and Latvia. Each principality elected their Diets, which chose representatives to serve in the Reichstag in Berlin.

Greece became dominant in the Aegean area, conquering Thrace and western Anatolia. The Greeks moved their capital from Athens to Constantinople. The Greek Navy dominated the Aegean Sea, with the islands, including Crete incorporated into

Greece.

The Russian Empire became the Russian Federation. The Russian government also moved the capital from Petrograd to Moscow. The former Russian provinces of Georgia, Armenia, Azerbaijan, Finland, and Moldova became independent nations. Finland established its capital city at Helsinki and allied with the Nordic Union.

The Ottoman Empire ceased to exist. The provinces of Mesopotamia, The Hejaz, and Syria became independent kingdoms. The Kurds calved out a nation called Kurdistan, with its capital of Mosul. Anatolia became the heartland of the new Republic of Turkey.

A new Caliph, Hussein bin Ali replaced the Sultan as the religious leader of Islam. Two of his sons ruled in Mesopotamia and Syria. The only threat to his authority came from the Saud Kingdom in central Arabia. He was confident that if the Saudi's proved troublesome, the armies of Hejaz, Syria, and Mesopotamia, equipped with modern weapons would defeat them.

A new decade dawned from the ruins of war. Millions of civilians faced starvation and disease. The Bird Flu which swept the world from 1918 to 1920 took the lives of fifty to one-hundred million civilians. That was estimated to be three times the amount of total deaths attributed to the war. Death totals in areas untouched by the war comprised up to six percent of the population. Many of the infections came from soldiers returning home from the war or moving to other countries. In the United States, almost one million persons died.

By 1921, the pandemic abated. Unscarred by war, the United States emerged as the most powerful nation in the world. She dominated all of North America, and with the Panama Canal and the naval base in Chimbote Bay, Peru influenced South American national priorities.

Looking around the world for potential adversaries, the Naval war College focused on the Empire of Japan; which expanded its influence by appropriating the former German colonies in China, The Marshall and Caroline Islands. The expanding military bases in those islands became a potential threat to United States possessions in the Philippines, Guam, Wake, and Hawaii.

Secretly, the Naval War College war-gamed various scenarios of a war with the Empire of Japan. The results were mixed. Japan's smaller fleet consolidated itself near the home islands. The positioning of the Pacific Fleet included task forces in Bremerton, Washington, Mare Island, and Long Beach California, Chimbote Bay and Pearl Harbor. That dispersal's design was to project power in multiple locations, with minimal threat to the fleet. With a threat of war, the fleet could consolidate.

The Panama Canal allowed for quick access for reinforcements to either the Atlantic or Pacific fleets. Groups influenced by the doctrines of Alfred Thayer Mahan advocated for newer and larger battleships to project seapower. Others promoted more aircraft carriers to serve as seaborne airports to obtain intelligence from remote areas and to project air power into a war. Billy Mitchel's aviators previously convincingly proved that airpower could sink a pre-Dreadnought target battleship with bombs.

The Naval War College postulated a middle road. A written report to the Department of the Navy proposed a new class of fast battleships capable of speeds more than thirty knots, which would allow the warships to keep up with and protect a fleet of the fast aircraft carriers.

The War College recommendations influenced the Department of the Navy to request the set-aside funds to convert the two other Lexington Class battlecruiser hulls to be the prototypes of the new generation of Missouri Class fast battleships. The first two carried the names USS Missouri and the USS New Jersey. The new class would incorporate the advances of the South Dakota Class into a longer hull with larger electric turbine engines. The estimated hull speed of the Missouri Class fast battleships was 33 knots. A standard design would economize costs, and allow for modifications as technology improved.

Afterword

The second book in this series, World Power, postulated a growing super-power in the Western Hemisphere, which drastically changed United States history. The annexation of Canada allowed for the admission of additional states. The domination of the Caribbean provided for mass emigration of southern blacks to Cuba, Puerto Rico and Dominica. This migration also eliminated the scourge of southern white discrimination against the black population living in the south. The policies of *Jim Crow* and *Separate but Equal* do not happen in my timeline.

Book three postulates how the strength of the United States Navy enabled it to establish a naval base at Chimbote Bay in Peru. The defeat of Chile at Chimbote Bay established United States hegemony in

South America.

In actual history, Peru offered to lease Chimbote Bay to the United States. Chile prevented as she possessed a modern navy with ironclad battleships, constructed in Great Britain. The United States Post-Civil War navy was allowed to decline to steam-powered wood frigates and sloops. These warships would not have survived a battle with the Chilian Navy.

The next significant change in history came with the delayed assassination of President McKinley. The timing allowed for Teddy Roosevelt to serve two full terms. Instead of the historical feud between Roosevelt and Taft in the Republican Party in 1912, Roosevelt provided enthusiastic cooperation. Woodrow Wilson did not become President, as he battled with a united Republican Party.

I also changed the scenario of the beginning of The Great War. The assassination attempt on Arch Duke Francis Ferdinand in

Sarajevo failed. The ArchDuke was a reformer, and much out of favor with Emperor Franz Joseph, who rejoiced after the actual assassination.

I also flipped the Battle of Dogger Bank, with a change in command of the German Navy. An aggressive Admiral Scheer replaced the timid Admiral Ingenohl. Actual history records that Admiral Ingenohl missed a golden opportunity for victory by retreating in the face of inferior Royal Navy forces.

An analogy is the replacement of Admiral Bull Halsey with Admiral Fletcher just before the Battle of Midway. Admiral Yamamoto predicated his strategy on the presumption that Bull Halsey would charge directly into a superior battleship fleet. Instead, Admiral Fletcher contented himself with the destruction of four Japanese fleet carriers.

In my version, the Royal Navy's defeat at Dogger Bank, and the formation of the Nordic Union motivated the Royal Navy's occupation of Narvik, Norway. Paranoia resulted from the loss of so many dreadnoughts in one battle. The invasion soured American public opinion, mainly the Irish against Great Britain.

I also postulated a Taft Doctrine of Peace Through Strength, which kept the United States out of the war. He actively built up the United States Navy to defend the 3,000 miles width of the Atlantic Ocean. The policy was not isolationism, as the United States State Department actively pursued peace initiatives.

Without the United States entry, the Triple Entente could not defeat the Central Powers. The French Army was in mutiny with thousands deserting daily. The German Armies exhausted themselves. Compounding the issues, the economies of all the warring nations, devastated by the prolonged war faced catastrophe.

King Albert of Belgium proposed a policy of no winners – no losers in the war. He was ignored by the British and French.

After the defeat of the Russians, The Kaiser offered a similar solution to end the conflict as did King Albert's on the Western Front. Had the United States stayed out of the war, a ceasefire and subsequent treaties closely resembling what I postuated at Breton Woods might have happened.

I followed the Russian Revolution from the beginning. I twisted it with the capture and execution of Stalin and Trotsky during the Petrograd uprising in July 1917. Lenin's defeat, capture, and exchange for the Royal Family in 1918 is a sound theory. If Germany was not defeated in the Great War, an intervention to prevent a Bolshevik victory is a distinct possibility. In real-time, the belated response by Western Powers in Russia, and by Japan in the Far East failed to prevent the Bolshevik victory.

The deaths of the exiled Tsar and Tsarevich from the Bird Flu could have happened. An estimated fifty to one-hundred million died in this worldwide pandemic.

The dissolution of the Ottoman Empire was inevitable. In real-time, the British occupation of Mesopotamia and the Hejaz, and French occupation of Syria and Lebanon resulted in the Sykes-Picot agreement which created the modern middle east. In my timeline, organic revolutions precipitated the fall of the Ottomans; thus the future of the middle-east is open for change.

In real-time, the Greeks conquered eastern Anatolia until 1922. A united Nationalist Turkey, led by Kemal Ataturk, drove them out and reclaimed Constantinople, and renamed it Istanbul. The Turks slaughtered tens of thousands of Greek and Armenian minority populations.

Reviews are critical to authors. In electronic media, they promote more advertising for the book, resulting in additional sales. If you enjoyed reading this and the other books I have written, please leave me a review with your comments.

Thank you,

Brian Boyington

Made in the USA
Monee, IL
17 October 2020